SO-BMR-574

NEW YORK REVIEW BOOKS
CLASSICS

THE WIDOW

GEORGES SIMENON (1903–1989) was born in Liège,
Belgium. He went to work as a reporter at the age of fifteen
and in 1923 moved to Paris, where under various pseudonyms he became a highly successful and prolific author of
pulp fiction while leading a dazzling social life. In the early
1930s, Simenon emerged as a writer under his own name,
gaining renown for his detective stories featuring Inspector
Maigret. He also began to write his psychological novels,
or *romans durs*—books in which he displays a sympathetic
awareness of the emotional and spiritual pain underlying
the routines of daily life. Having written nearly two hundred books under his own name and become the best-selling
author in the world, Simenon retired as a novelist in 1973,
devoting himself instead to dictating several volumes of
memoirs.

PAUL THEROUX is a novelist and travel writer who di-
vides his time between Cape Cod and Hawaii. Among his
books are the novels *The Mosquito Coast*, *Millroy the
Magician*, and *My Secret History* and the travel memoirs
Dark Star Safari, *Riding the Iron Rooster*, and *The Great
Railway Bazaar*. He has edited *The Best American Travel
Writing* and in 2007 published three novellas collected as
The Elephanta Suite.

THE WIDOW

GEORGES SIMENON

Translated from the French by
JOHN PETRIE

Introduction by
PAUL THEROUX

NEW YORK REVIEW BOOKS

New York

HALF HOLLOW HILLS
COMMUNITY LIBRARY

THIS IS A NEW YORK REVIEW BOOK
PUBLISHED BY THE NEW YORK REVIEW OF BOOKS
435 Hudson Street, New York, NY 10014
www.nyrb.com

Copyright © 1942 Georges Simenon Limited (a Chorion company)
Introduction copyright © 2008 by Paul Theroux
All rights reserved.

Library of Congress Cataloging-in-Publication Data

Simenon, Georges, 1903–1989.
  [Veuve Couderc. English]
  The widow / by Georges Simenon ; introduction by Paul Theroux ; translated
by John Petrie.
      p. cm. — (New York Review Books classics)
  ISBN 978-1-59017-261-2 (alk. paper)
  I. Petrie, John. II. Title.
PQ2637.I53V4513 2008
843'.912—dc22

                                    2007047811

ISBN 978-1-59017-261-2

Printed in the United States of America on acid-free paper.
10 9 8 7 6 5 4 3 2 1

INTRODUCTION

TWO STARTLINGLY similar short novels appeared in France in 1942, at the center of each narrative, a conscienceless and slightly creepy young man, unattached and adrift, perpetrator of a meaningless murder. One was Camus' *L'Étranger*, the other Simenon's *La veuve Couderc*. Camus' novel rose to become part of the literary firmament, and is still glittering, intensely studied, and praised—to my mind, overpraised. Simenon's novel did not drop but settled, so to speak, went the way of the rest of his work—rattled along with decent sales, the occasional reprint, and was even resurrected as a 1950s pulp-fiction paperback with a come-on tag line ("A surging novel of torment and desire") and a lurid cover: busty peasant girl pouting in a barn, her skirt hiked over her knees, while a hunky guy lurks at the door— price twenty-five cents.

Camus had labored for years on his novel of alienation; his *Carnets* record his frustration and false starts. "The fewer novels or plays you write—because of other parasitic interests—the fewer you will have the ability to write," V. S. Pritchett once wrote, lamenting his own small fictional output. "The law ruling the arts is that they must be pursued to excess." Simenon had published three other novels in 1942, and six the previous year. *La veuve Couderc* (in English variously *The Widow* and *Ticket of Leave*) became another title on the extremely long list of Simenon works; none of them regarded as a subject for scholarship.

If reading Camus represents duty, Simenon represents indulgence, a lavishness that seems frivolous, inspiring a greedy satisfaction that shows as self-consciousness in even the most well-intentioned introductions to his work, the critic's awkwardness over a pleasurable text, together with a shiver of snooty superfluity and the palpable cringe, common to many introducers of a Simenon novel, What am I doing here?

Simenon takes some sorting out, because at first glance he seems easily classified and on second thought (after you have read fifty or sixty of his books) unclassifiable. The Camus comparison is not gratuitous—Simenon often made it himself, and André Gide brought the same subject up a few years after *L'Étranger* appeared, favoring Simenon's work, especially this novel. And (in a 1947 letter to Albert Guerard) he went further, calling Simenon "*notre plus grand romancier aujourd'hui, vrai romancier.*"

Born ten years apart, both Camus and Simenon had arrived raw and youthful in metropolitan France from the distant margins of literary Francophonia—Camus a French Algerian and polemical journalist with a philosophical bent, Simenon a self-educated Belgian who began his writing life as a cub reporter with a taste for crime stories; the pedant and the punk, both with an eye for the ladies. Camus seems to have taken no notice of Simenon (no mention at all in any Camus biography), though we know that Simenon was watchful and somewhat competitive with the decade-younger Camus, whose complete works (he must have noted) can be accommodated between the covers of one modest-sized volume. The indefatigable Simenon, confident of winning the Nobel Prize, predicted in 1937 that he would win it in within ten years. The literature prize went to others—Pearl S. Buck, F. E. Sillanpää, Winston S. Churchill. Hearing the news in 1957 that Camus had won it, Simenon (so his wife reported) became enraged. "Can you believe that asshole got it and not me?"

What to make of the gifted and unstoppable writer who has a rarified existential streak but also a nose for what the public wants? The universities are seldom any help—no one is less welcome in the literature departments than the accomplished filler of multiple shelves of books. Like many self-educated people, Simenon tended to be anti-intellectual in a defiant and mocking way, despising literary critics and giving literature departments a wide berth. The universities returned the compliment, rubbishing him and belittling or ignoring his work. The academy is uncommonly fond of the struggler and the sufferer; scratch even the most severe academic and you find an underdogger. How can (so the argument seems to run) a prolific and popular writer be any good? Usually, like Ford Madox Ford or Trollope, they are nailed as graphomaniacs and subjected to cruel simplification, represented by one book, not always their best.

Professorial philistinism dogged Simenon; so did snobbery. And it was after all a bitter, provincial university librarian who wrote of

> ... the shit in the shuttered château
> Who does his five hundred words,
> Then parts out the rest of the day
> Between bathing and booze and birds ...

Simenon was the living intimidating embodiment of Philip Larkin's envious lines, plenty of booze and birds available, though his daily output in the château was more like 5,000 words.

Simenon considered himself the equal of Balzac. He regarded his novels as a modern-day *Comédie humaine*. His one foray into literary criticism was a long and insightful essay on Balzac, which took the form of mother-blaming. "A novelist is a man who does not like his mother, or who never received mother-love," words that applied equally to himself and that inform one of his memoirs, *Letter to My Mother*. He was the Balzac of blighted lives, writing out of a suffering that was not obvious until the end of his long career. Material success, one of Balzac's major themes, is not a theme that interested Simenon, who dwelled on failure, in spite of the fact that he himself was a great success and made a point of crowing about it.

Incredibly, for such a productive soul, Simenon was at times afflicted with writer's block, and though in Simenon it seemed almost an affectation, it perturbed him to the extent that he used it as an occasion to keep a diary, to recapture his novel-writing mood. In the diary he recounted his obsessional subjects—money, his family, his mother, the household, and other writers. During the writing of this diary, Henry Miller visited him and extravagantly praised him as someone who lived an enviable life. While Simenon humored him, and anatomized his character, he unblocked himself with this unusual and valuable journal, later published under the title *When I Was Old.*

His many straight detective novels based on the character of Chief Inspector Jules Maigret fit a pattern, as compact case studies, problems of lingering guilt and subtle clues, with a shrewd even lovable detective of settled habits. He came up with the rounded and believable and happily married Maigret in 1930 and did not stop adding to that shelf until 1972, seventy-six volumes later. But what about the rest of the books? The immensity of Simenon's life and letters baffles and defeats the simplifier. How to square the years in Liège as a reporter and an admitted hack with his postwar retreat to rural Connecticut? The trip through the Pacific in 1935, with the year he dropped out to travel by barge through France? The Arizona novels? The many châteaux? The classic cars he collected? The gourmandizing, the womanizing? "Most people work every day and enjoy sex periodically. Simenon had sex every day and every few months indulged in a frenzied orgy of work," writes

Patrick Marnham, in *The Man Who Wasn't Maigret*. Simenon lived long enough to have made love to Josephine Baker and to stare priapically into the cleavage of Brigitte Bardot. What of his ability to write a chapter a day and finish an excellent novel in a ten or eleven days, and write another one a few months later?

Simenon's detractors put him down as a compulsive hack; to his admirers, who included not just the hard-to-impress Henry Miller and the sniffily Olympian Gide, as well as the generally aloof Thornton Wilder and the quite remote Jorge Amado, he was the consummate writer. He had no time for his other contemporaries. It wasn't a question of his believing he was better than any of them; he simply took no notice of them. Even at the height of his friendship with Henry Miller, he did not read Miller's work; he suggested it was unreadable, but shrewdly analyzed Miller the man in *When I Was Old*. He claimed in *The Paris Review* to have been inspired by Gogol and Dostoyevsky, but he wrote nothing insightful about them.

Like many other writers he hated anyone probing into his life, and habitually lied, laid false trails, or exaggerated his experiences. In 1932, he traveled through central Africa. Typically, he claimed he had been in Africa a year. The actual time was two months. Never mind, he made the best of it and wrote three novels with African settings. He hid himself, never more than when he was promoting one of his books, as the dapper writer, puffing his pipe, obscuring himself with phenomenal statistics. But the statistics were misleading in the way that record-breaking is misleading, merely the helpless adoration of the exceptional. Simenon trotting out his big numbers sounds to me like a man's mendacious reckoning, not different from the modestly endowed group of islanders in Vanuatu who wear enormous phallocrypts and call themselves Big Nambas.

Yet, though they invite suspicion, the most unlikely figures associated with Simenon are probably true, the roundabout four hundred works of fiction he claimed to have published are verifiable. A hundred and seventeen are serious novels, the rest Maigrets and books written under pseudonyms. He dropped out of school at thirteen to become a reporter. The facts associated with him take such an extravagant form that he seems a victim of his own stupendous statistics—the numerous novels, the 500 million copies sold, the 55 changes of address, and his often quoted boast that he bedded 10,000 women. (His second wife put the figure at "no more than 1,200.")

It is perhaps not surprising that such a freakish example of creative energy is not seriously studied (though there exists a Centre d'Études Georges Simenon at the University of Liège). Apart from the Nobel omission, Simenon did not feel slighted. He said, "Writing is not a profession but a vocation of unhappiness." But the consequence is that every new reissue of a Simenon merits an introduction like this, because he seems (like many of his characters) to come from nowhere. Well, he agreed. He said that as a Belgian he was like a man without a country.

Though he claimed that none of his books was autobiographical, his work is a chronicle of his life—his young self is vivid in *Pedigree* and *The Nightclub*, his mother looms in *The Lodger* and *The Cat*, his daughter in *The Disappearance of Odile*, his second marriage in *Three Bedrooms in Manhattan*, his ménage a trios in *In Case of Emergency*, his travels in the novels with foreign settings—*Tropic Moon, Aboard the Aquitaine, Banana Tourist, The Bottom of the Bottle, Red Lights, The Brothers Rico*, and many others—and in all of them the particularities of his fantasies and obsessions. Feeling that he was an outsider, he had a gift for depicting aliens—the nameless African in *The Negro*, the immigrant in *The Little Man from Arkangel*, the Malous (in fact the Malowskis) in *The Fate of the Malous*, and Kachoudas in *The Hatter's Phantoms*. By contrast, in Camus' *The Plague* you'd hardly know you were in a foreign country—all the characters are Frenchmen, and incidentally *The Plague* is a world without women.

"You know you have a beautiful sentence, cut it," Simenon said. "Every time I find such a thing in one my novels it is to be cut." Simenon is exaggerating, he sometimes lets slip a pretty sentence, but generally his writing is so textureless as to be transparent and never calls attention to itself ("It's written as if by a child"). No love of language is ever obvious, he remains anti-lapidary. The only new words one is likely to find in Simenon are the occasional technical terms, like the medical jargon in *The Patient* with its medical terms, *The Premier* with its particularities of French governance, and some bridge-playing episodes elsewhere. You will never learn a new word in a Simenon. And you will never laugh. Comedy is absent, humor is rare. A bleak vision and relentless seriousness earned his non-Maigrets the appellation *romans durs* because *dur* is not just hard but implies weight, seriousness, not only a stony quality but density and complexity—a kind of challenge and even a certain tedium. (A *dur* is a bore in some contexts.) Simenon's characters read newspapers, usually bad news or crimes; they plot, lie, cheat, steal, sweat, have sex; frequently they commit murder, and just as often they commit suicide. They never read books or quote from them. They don't study (as Simenon did, to mug up on detail). They are generally fussing at the margins of the working world, coming apart, hurtling downward, toward oblivion.

For any writer, it is not possible to be productive without being possessed by a strict sense of order and guided by discipline. One of Simenon's shrewdest French biographers, Pierre Assouline, sees the clock as his dominant metaphor. His novels are full of timepieces and clock-watching. Simenon himself timed all his movements, not just his writing, clocking in, clocking out; even meals were timed to the minute. He famously made calendars chronicling his novel writing—usually eight or nine days of furious composition, a chapter a day.

His sexuality, too, involved the stopwatch. Simenon was

anything but a sensualist. A sex act in his books usually takes a few lines at most. In *The Bells of Bicetre*: "They stayed a long time almost motionless, like certain insects you see mating." *The Man on the Bench in the Barn*: "I literally dived into her, suddenly, violently, there was fear in her eyes"—and then it's over. *The Nightclub*: "She looked at him in astonishment. It was over already. He couldn't even have said how he set about it."

These hair-trigger instances echo the love life Simenon recorded in his *Intimate Memoirs*. One day, he approaches his wife in her office as she is speaking with her English secretary, Joyce Aitken. His wife asks him what he wants.

> "You!"
> That afternoon she simply lies down on the rug.
> "Hurry up. You don't have to leave, Aitken."

The Widow is exceptional in depicting several seductions that go on for a few pages. A sentence that repeats so often in a Simenon as to be a signature line is: "She wore a dress and it was obvious that she had nothing on underneath." *The Widow* also contains a variation of this sentence: "Still wearing her blue smock, with next to nothing beneath it . . ."

Unlike most of his characters, Simenon was someone whose self-esteem was in good repair. His personal world seemed complete. He moved from grand house to grand house—and they were self-contained, holding his family, his lovers, his library, his recreations; his appetites, his pipes, his pencils, his fancy cars. He lived the life of a seigneur, the lord of his own principality, where everything was ordered to his own specifications. The completeness of Simenon's life is impressive: the man who lives with his ex-wife, his present wife, and his loyal servant, all of whom he sleeps with, while still finding time to be unfaithful to all three with prostitutes, and keeps writing.

That was what thrilled Henry Miller. Well, what philanderer wouldn't be thrilled? And Miller didn't know the half of it. One day (according to Marnham), seeing a young serving girl on all fours dusting a low table, Simenon on an impulse took her from behind. The girl told Madame Simenon, who laughed it off as being typically Georges. Witnessing this drollery, another serving girl wondered aloud, "*On passe toutes a la casserole?*" ("So everyone has a go at this pot?")

In great contrast to the apparent coherence, the fatness, of his own life are the insufficiencies in the lives of his characters, who are usually strong enough to kill but seldom resourceful enough to survive. And it must be said that having spent many decades vigorously writing and living in style, his last years, twenty-three of them—after the suicide of his beloved daughter—were spent in a kind of solitary confinement and protracted depression in a poky house with his housekeeper, sitting in plastic chairs because, among his phobias, he held the belief that wooden furniture harbored insects.

A number of Simenon's novels, among them *The Venice Train*, *Belle*, *Sunday*, and *The Negro*, can be grouped around the general theme *malentendu* or cross-purposes—the title of the Camus play that is Simenonesque in its cruelty. *The Widow* is firmly in this category, though its descriptions of violence and sexuality are unusually graphic for Simenon; and it is one of the few Simenons with a strong woman character in it. The woman in *Betty* and the woman narrator of *November* are similarly strong. But his women tend to be one-dimensional, guileful, opportunistic, coldly practical, unsentimental, or else easy prey. Tati the widow is a peasant who knows her own mind and possesses an ability to size up strangers.

The action takes place in the Bourbonnais, the dead center of France, in a hamlet by the canal that joins St. Amande with

Montluçon—apart from omitting the "e" from Amande, Simenon is very specific in his provincial geography.

An odd solecism occurs in the first paragraph of the novel. A man is walking down a road that is "cut slantwise every ten yards by the shadow of a tree trunk"—Simenon at his most economical in precise description. It is noontime, at the end of May. The man strides across these shadows. Then his own shadow is described: "a short, ridiculously squat shadow—his own—slid in front of him." The sun seems to be shining from different angles in the space of two sentences, creating two sorts of shadow. It is perhaps not a riddle. Simenon hated to rewrite.

The young man boards the bus outside St. Amande, bound for Montluçon. He has nothing on him, no impedimenta, no obvious identity. "No luggage, no packages, no walking stick, not even a switch cut from the hedge. His arms swung freely." Among the women returning from the market he is a stranger, though for the reader of Simenon he is so familiar as to be an old friend: the naked man, someone at a crossroads, a bit lost, a bit guilty, on the verge of making a fatal decision.

The widow Couderc sizes him up, seeing something in him no one else sees. Later we understand why: he somewhat resembles her son, a waster and ex-con who is in the Foreign Legion. She sees that this bus passenger is going nowhere, that he has nothing; she understands him and she wants him.

In this beautifully constructed first chapter, with a subtle building of effects, the young man notices the woman, too, and in the midst of the nosy chattering market women, the two "recognized each other." He also needs her.

The woman, Tati, gets off the bus, and soon afterward the young man, Jean, does the same. Jean asks if he can give her a hand with her bundles, a gesture she had been expecting ever since their eyes met. He moves in with her. A few days later, on a Sunday, after she returns from church—a nice touch—she pours him a few drinks and they end up in bed.

She is not beautiful, but she is tough, even fearless, the sort of indestructible peasant who would feel at home at the table in van Gogh's *The Potato Eaters*. Unloved and frumpy, even slatternly, in an old ragged coat, her slip showing, and with a hairy mole on her cheek, she is at forty-five more than twenty years older than Jean. She gives Jean to understand that he can expect occasional sex but that she must also sleep with her abusive father-in-law from time to time, because she is living in his farmhouse.

Belying Tati's rumpled clothes, and precarious existence among her quarrelsome in-laws, is her animal alertness, a peasant shrewdness, especially as regards her niece. The teenaged mother Felicie lives nearby; the effect of this pretty young woman on Jean disturbs Tati. Her suspicions of Jean's past are quickly borne out after a visit by the gendarmes: Jean has recently been released from five years in prison (thus the *Ticket of Leave* title) and his precariousness resembles hers. She had taken him for a foreigner—he seems foreign throughout, a true outsider—but in fact he is from a distinguished family in Montluçon, son of a wealthy womanizing distiller. Estranged from his family, he is "free as air... a man utterly without ties." And "he was free... like a child."

"He did not walk like other people. He seemed to be going nowhere." But he has walked into a trap. He does not know it yet, though for him, as for Meursault in *L'Étranger*, there is no future. He lives in a "magnificent present humming with sunshine."

He tells Tati that he has murdered a man, almost casually and partly by accident. A woman was involved, though he didn't love her. Far from being seriously affected by the crime, the trial, or the years in prison, he "scarcely realized that it was himself it was happening to." He has been cast adrift by the crime, and after prison nothing mattered: "he was committed to nothing, nothing he did possessed either weight or importance."

In his lack of remorse, or pity, he resembles the cold-hearted killer Frank Friedmaier in *Dirty Snow* and Popinga in *The Man Who Watched Trains Go By*. And of course, he prefigures Meursault, even to the solar imagery, for at a crucial point in the novel, recognizing his desire for Felicie, "At one stroke the sun had taken possession of him. Another world was swallowing them up..."

He succeeds with Felicie, as he succeeded with her aunt, but wordlessly, rutting among the farm buildings. He continues to make love to Tati, and is always abrupt if not brutal: "He undressed her as one skins a rabbit." And in this ménage, another familiar Simenon situation ensues, that of lovers separated by a physical barrier, the passions of propinquity, jealousy always figuring in the plot. In *The Widow* the lovers in nearby cottages are separated by the canal, in *The Door* a communicating door, in *The Iron Staircase* an iron staircase, and a similar shuttling back and forth in *Act of Passion*. All these novels end in murder.

In this springtime pastoral—conflict in the countryside: fertile farmland, browsing animals, quarreling peasants—Jean slowly goes to pieces, consumed by self-disgust and fatalism. Typically for Simenon, by the subtle building of effects, Jean's condition is suggested rather than analyzed. Feeling possessed by the desperate older woman who won't let him go, by the younger woman who is indifferent to him, Jean realizes that he is at a dead end, that a crime is inevitable, and "he waited for what could not fail to happen."

The novel becomes implicitly existential, though Simenon would scoff at such a word: there is no philosophical meditation in the narrative. Jean has been put on a road to ruin by Simenon—been set up, indeed. Many if not all Simenon novels describing the occurrence of *malentendu* imply that there is no exit—and the maddening thing is that even though the doomed character does not see a way out, the reader does. It does not occur to Jean that he can just walk away or get back on the bus. He protests that he is indifferent to his crime, but he is damaged, he is guilt-ridden, he is possessed, and when Tati begs him to stay and love her, he is helpless to do anything but smash her skull. "It had been foreordained!"

In describing this lost soul and his desperate act, Simenon was reflecting the fatalism of his time. He wrote the book in a dark period, on the French coast—the name "Nieul sur Mer" is given at the end as its place of composition, a place near La Rochelle. France was at war, German occupation not far off, and doomsday seemed imminent. In this uncertain war, only violence or an act of passion gave meaning to the passage of time. Like Meursault, Jean is headed to certain execution—the notion of it occurs to him throughout the last third of the novel—and he is the author of his fate. He had stumbled into an idyllic setting without at first realizing that it was not idyllic at all but an Eden that has become a snake pit of corruption matching his own loss of innocence.

Rereading the novel, one realizes that (as with most Simenons), Jean had been doomed from the first paragraph, when he walked through the shadows. And we can easily see why Simenon was so angry that Camus won the Swedish lottery—because in novel after novel, Simenon dramatized the same sort of dilemma, the life with narrowing options (but always with subtle differences of plot, tone, location, and effects), the risk-taking of the man with nothing to lose, his vanity, his presumption, his willful self-destruction. Earlier, Jean yearns for commitment and for fate to intervene, but when he meditates on it (and ultimately gets his wish): "He wanted something definite and final, something that offered no prospect of retreat." Simenon seems to be talking to himself, sending another of his characters to his death in a world without happy endings.

—PAUL THEROUX

THE WIDOW

I

A MAN WALKING. One man, on a stretch of road three miles long cut slantwise every ten yards by the shadow of a tree trunk, striding unhurriedly from one shadow to the next. As it was almost noon, with the sun nearly at its highest point, a short, ridiculously squat shadow—his own—slid in front of him.

The dead-straight road climbed to the top of a long slope, where it seemed to stop short. To the left there were crackling sounds in the wood. To the right, in the fields swelling like breasts, there was nothing but a horse a long way off, a horse drawing a cask mounted on wheels; and in the same field a scarecrow which might perhaps be a man.

At that moment the red bus was leaving St. Amand, where it was market day, forcing its way with blasts of the horn. At last it left the endless street of white houses and started along the two rows of roadside elms. It picked up one more woman, waiting with her umbrella up because of the sun. There was no room to sit. The woman did not think of setting down her baskets, but stood swaying between the seats, and staring like a sick hen.

"It was Jeanine—she was in the next box—who told me, and she even was disgusted.... And when Jeanine's disgusted!..."

The driver sat impassively, wearing his official cap and his mauve tie rather askew, looking straight ahead at the dark lines striped across the road. No smoking. The sign was up. The cigarette stuck to his lip was out.

"I know...." he uttered in the tone of one who knows what he is talking about.

And the big girl who, fifteen minutes before the bus was to leave had settled herself in the seat next to the driver, went on, punctuating her whispered story with giggles, "There was Léon, the hairdresser.... And Lolotte...And a boy from Montluçon who works at the airplane factory.... Then there was Rose...."

"Which Rose?"

"You must know her. You meet her every day on the road, on a bicycle. She's the daughter of the butcher at Tilly. A fat girl with scarlet cheeks and eyes popping out of her head who wears her dresses too short. She goes to St. Amand to learn shorthand and typing.... A real bitch!"

Ducks and chickens were stirring in their baskets. Forty women, perhaps more, all dressed in black, were squashed into the seats, and most of them sat silent and staring, their heads, along with the motion of the bus, swayed from left to right while every now and then all their bosoms lunged forward.

Ten, nine, eight miles farther along the man was still walking on, like someone going nowhere in particular with nothing particular in mind. No luggage, no packages, no walking stick, not even a switch cut from the hedge. His arms swung freely.

"Léon began with Lolotte, and she was laughing so loud that the people in the movie kept telling them to be quiet."

The big red bus was drawing nearer. A gray car overtook it. Not local people. They came from far, and they had far to go. The car was traveling fast. It started up the slope. The walking man heard its approach without slackening his pace; he merely turned his head a little and raised one arm, with no great hope of success.

The car did not stop. The woman beside the driver asked, "What did he want?"

Turning around, she saw a tall silhouette still moving from

the shadow of one tree trunk to the shadow of the next, then almost at once the car was over the top and going down the slope on the other side.

The bus followed, rumbling in low gear. It vibrated more than ever. The widow Couderc, behind the driver, kept glancing anxiously upward, as the packages on top of the bus could be heard rattling about.

The man on the road raised his arm once again. The bus pulled up just by him. The driver, keeping his seat, opened the door with a familiar movement.

"Where to?"

The man looked around him and mumbled, as though it were the most natural thing in the world, "I don't mind. Where are you heading for?"

"Montluçon..."

"That'll do."

"Montluçon? Eight francs..."

The bus started off again. Standing inside, the man hunted through his pockets, fetching out a five-franc piece, then a two-franc bit, and finally, after searching his other pockets without any particular anxiety, found another fifty centimes.

"Here's seven francs fifty. I'll get out a bit before Montluçon."

The old wives on their way back from market looked at him. The widow Couderc looked at him, but not in the same way as the rest of them. The girl sitting by the driver looked at him too: she had never met a man like this before.

The bus was laboring up the last of the slope. Little puffs of cool air came in through the open windows. The widow Couderc had a lock of hair hanging over her brow, her bun was on the point of falling down and her pink slip—a queer bluish pink—showed under the hem of her dress.

There was a sound of bells, but the church could not be seen. It must be midday. A house loomed at the side of the road, and a woman got out of the bus opposite the doorstep where two children sat.

It was odd: there were forty passengers, and only one of them, the widow Couderc, looked at the man any differently from the way you would look at just anybody. The rest were placid and quiet, like cows in a meadow watching a wolf browsing in their midst without the least astonishment.

And yet he was a man such as they had never seen in this bus which took them to market each Saturday. The widow Couderc had sensed this at the very first glance. She had seen him thumb the car before he stopped the bus. She had noticed that he was empty-handed; and you just don't walk empty-handed along the main road without so much as knowing where you're going.

She was not forgetting to keep a lookout for the antics of the packages on the roof, but all the same she did not take her eyes off him, and she took note of everything—his stubbly cheeks, his pale, unseeing eyes, his gray suit, worn yet having a touch of ease about it, his thin shoes. A man who could walk noiselessly and spring like a cat. And who, after the seven francs fifty he had given to the driver in exchange for a blue ticket, probably had no money left in his pockets.

He was watching her, too, screwing up his eyes as if to see her better, and from time to time he pursed up his lips as though smiling to himself. Perhaps he was amused at widow Couderc's wen. Everyone called it "the wen." It was on her left cheek, a spot the size of a five-franc piece, a spot covered with hundreds of brown, silky hairs, as if a piece of animal's hide, a marten say, had been grafted there.

The bus was now going down the other slope, and behind the trees there were occasional glimpses of the river Cher, its lively water leaping over the stones.

Widow Couderc too hugged a secret smile. The man blinked

slightly. It was rather as if, in the midst of all these old women with their nodding heads, the two had recognized each other.

She almost forgot that she had reached her stop. She realized suddenly that they were at the foot of the hill. She leaned forward, tapped the driver on the back, and he braked.

"Have to give me a hand with my incubator!" she said.

She was short and broad, rather plump. It was quite a business getting out of the bus with all her baskets: at one moment she wanted to get out first herself, the next she wanted to put her baskets down on the road first.

The driver jumped down. The thirty or forty women in the bus watched her without a word. There was a little house not far off, a tiny two-roomed house with a blue-painted fence around it.

"Mind you don't break anything. Those things can't take much handling!"

The driver had climbed up the iron ladder at the back and onto the roof of the bus and now he lowered a kind of enormous box with four feet. The widow Couderc took it and set it very cautiously at the side of the road.

She took a two-franc piece out of a full purse, and handed it to him. "There, young man..."

But it was the man they had picked up from the road that she eyed, with a shade of regret.

The bus started off again. Through the rear window the man could see the widow Couderc standing at the roadside, beside her enormous box and her baskets.

"Just like her niece," said the big girl next to the driver. "Do you know Félicie?..."

The man could have sat down now that there was a seat empty. He kept standing. The road curved. Widow Couderc and the little house disappeared.... Then he too leaned forward and tapped the driver's shoulder.

"Drop me here, will you?"

When the bus moved on, all heads turned to watch him making off in the opposite direction, and the girl confided her impression to the driver: "Queer fish!"

He was already farther along than he had thought. It took him several minutes before he saw the little house once more, the packages at the roadside and widow Couderc, who had opened the gate and was knocking at the door.

She was not surprised to see him coming. She moved toward the gate as he came to a halt.

"I thought the Bichat woman would be at home and would lend me her wheelbarrow!" she said. "And now look, everything's shut."

All the same, she called out in a shrill voice, turning different ways, "Clémence!... Clémence!..."

Then: "I wonder where she can be. She never goes out. She must have had bad news about her sister...."

She walked around the house, banged on another closed door.

"If only I could find her wheelbarrow!"

But there was nothing but the vegetable patch and a few flowers. No wheelbarrow. A turtledove in a cage.

"Do you live far from here?" asked the man.

"Less than half a mile, by the canal. I was counting on Clémence's wheelbarrow...."

"Would you like me to give you a hand?"

She did not refuse. She had been expecting it.

"Do you think you'll be able to carry the incubator all by yourself? You'll have to be careful: it breaks easily."

And all the time she was darting little glances at him, curious, but already satisfied.

"It's a bargain. I saw it in front of the hardware store, just as I got to market. I offered him two hundred francs. It wasn't until I was getting right into the bus that he let me have it for three hundred. It's not too heavy?"

It was unwieldy, but not heavy. Things shifted inside the box.

"Look out—there's a lamp. . . ."

She followed, carrying her baskets. They turned into a side road, edged with hazels and filled with soft shade: the ground underfoot was yielding, as in a wood.

Drops of sweat stood out on the man's brow.

"Looking for work?" she said, hurrying to catch up with him, for he walked quickly.

He made no answer. His shirt was beginning to stick to his body. His hands were so damp he was afraid he might lose his hold.

"Wait while I go and open the door. . . ."

The door was already open, leading to a rather large kitchen. Coming in from outside, they could not at first see anything in the dim light.

"Put that down here. Soon we'll . . ."

A ginger cat rubbed against her legs. She put down her baskets on a pine table. Then she opened a second door, and the flood of sunshine from the garden invaded the room. As she passed, the man caught the whiff of her armpits.

"Sit down a moment. I'm going to get you a glass of wine."

What was wrong? She was uneasy, like an animal returning to its burrow and winding a strange scent. What made her notice some grease on the table top? It was scarcely visible. She looked up at the two hams hanging from a beam, and suddenly her eyes flared with anger.

"Wait! . . . Stay there. . . ."

She rushed into the garden, which looked like a farmyard, with a heap of manure, a cart propped on its shafts, chickens, geese, ducks.

Standing at the door, he watched her as she went. She walked like a woman who knows where she is going. He noticed someone else walking ahead of her, as though trying to get away, a young, thin girl, perhaps sixteen years old, with a baby on her arm.

The girl was making her way toward a gate beyond which was a hint of a canal and a drawbridge. She quickened her step. Widow Couderc walked faster. She caught up with the girl, and could be seen, but not heard, speaking vehemently, angrily.

The girl held the baby with one hand. The other was hidden beneath her blue-checked smock.

This was the hand which the widow dragged out, and from it she snatched a little package wrapped in a scrap of newspaper.

What sort of things would she be shouting at the fleeing girl? Insults, of course! And she slammed the gate shut. She came back with the parcel in her hand. She opened a door, the door of some shed out of which she pushed an old man who walked in front of her with dragging feet and lowered head.

"The bitch!" she exclaimed, coming back into the kitchen and dumping on the table two thick slices of ham that had been in the piece of newspaper.

"She took advantage of my being away again to come and see her grandfather and pinch some of my ham! You can't understand. . . . She's a little slut, that's what she is! Sixteen years old and got herself a baby already."

She glanced harshly at the old man, who was still standing there in the kitchen looking at nothing.

"And this old fool would give her everything there is in the house."

The old fool didn't move, just stared curiously at the box standing in the middle of the kitchen, part of it wrapped in brown paper.

"He's not proud, he isn't! He knows he'll pay for it! Look at the face he's pulling. . . ."

She opened a brown-painted cupboard, took out two glasses, showed them to the old man, and pushed a jug into his hand.

"He's deaf as a post. He can't even speak any more, not since he fell out of a hay wagon. An old piece of junk, that's what he is. . . . But when it comes to certain things he knows well enough how to act the lamb with Tati."

An excited flame had danced in her eyes and she looked the man over from head to foot.

"Tati's what I've been called since I was a child. I don't even know why. He's gone to draw some wine. . . . You're a foreigner, I'll bet?"

It was as if she were hesitating to take definite possession of him. She was still a little wary.

"No. I'm French."

"Oh! . . ."

Disappointment. She did not try to hide it.

"I could have sworn you were a foreigner. They pass this way sometimes, rather your style. The Chagots, at Drevant, had one for years, a Polack who used to sleep in the stable and could turn his hand to anything."

It was the man's turn to murmur: "Oh!"

"What's your name?"

"Jean."

All this time she was taking various things out of her baskets: two aprons, noodles, cans of sardines, a spool of black thread, a parcel of cold meat wrapped in wax paper. The old man came back with the jug full of ice-cold white wine.

"Why don't you sit down? . . . You wanted to get to Montluçon?"

"It's all one to me."

"To get a job in a factory, eh?"

She had stoked the stove and poured water into a pan.

"Ever worked an incubator before?"

"I think I'd know how."

"Wait while I go and feed the fowls. I think we might work out something."

She sat down to take off her shoes and put on a pair of black sabots. The pink slip—an odd electric, bluish pink—still showed under her dress, and it was impossible not to look at the patch of skin on her cheek, hairy and so silky.

"You can have a drink. Look at the old fool: he doesn't dare help himself because I just caught him with that bitch of a Félicie."

She poured out a drink for him. The old man was tall and thin, his face covered with a gray stubble, his eyes rimmed with red.

"You can have a drink, Couderc!" she shouted in his ear. "But when it comes to your bit of fun, you can wait quite a while yet. . . ."

How many times had she made the round of the kitchen already?

Yet there had not been a single wasted movement. The two slices of ham had been put away in a cupboard. Water was heating. The fire, livened up, was purring away. All the parcels she had brought back had been put away, and now she was going out with a basketful of grain.

"Chuck . . . chuck . . . chuck . . ."

He saw her, in the sun, by the cart leaning on its shafts, surrounded by at least a hundred chickens, all of them white, with ducks, geese, and turkeys by way of background.

"Chuck . . . chuck . . . chuck . . ."

She cast the grain in handfuls, like a sower, but she did not forget Jean standing framed in the doorway.

It was hot. The sun was so high there was scarcely any shade left. The old man had sat down in his corner by the hearth, and kept looking at the floor.

Beyond the fence which enclosed the garden, Jean saw a narrow boat, varnished like a toy, drawn by a donkey and gliding slowly along the canal. And since the canal was higher than the yard, there was the odd sight of a boat passing at head height. A little girl in red, with flaxen hair, was running along the deck. A woman was knitting, managing the tiller with her hips.

"You'll eat with us. Saturday, we don't put on anything much, on account of it being market day. Now, look at the old goat and tell me if it isn't bad luck...."

She set the table. Coarse, flowered china, tumblers of thick glass. She opened a can of sardines. There was some beef, too, and slices of sausage.

"Would you like an omelet?"

"Yes."

She was surprised. She had expected him to say no, out of politeness, and she smiled a secret smile.

The old man moved to the table and took a knife out of his pocket. In the glass clockcase a wide brass disk swung slowly to and fro. The cat jumped onto Jean's knee and was purring already.

"Push her on the floor if she worries you.... So you're a Frenchman? I'm not asking where you come from.... Do you like your omelet moist?"

She followed his gaze and saw his eye had been caught by an enlarged photograph of a soldier in the uniform of the African Battalion.

"It's René, my son," she said.

She was not ashamed of his being in the African Battalion. On the contrary! She looked at Jean as though to say, "You see, I understand...."

They ate. The old man did not count. On one side, the light reached them only through a tiny window looking onto the road and on the other it came, more vibrant, through the door open onto the yard.

"I was wondering whether you'd get as far as Montluçon."

"So was I. . . ."

"I manage singlehanded, mind you. Couderc..." She felt the need to explain, "that's the old trash. My late husband's father. Each as bad as the other. I was saying he's just about to take our two cows out to graze, and putter around. And one other thing besides, the old tomcat! Look at that face he's pulling! There's some who say he hears more than he lets on, but I know better."

She shouted, "Isn't it the truth, Couderc?"

He gave a start, but seemed not to understand. He just lowered his head over his plate.

"Couderc! Isn't it the truth that you're an old tomcat, and that you used to chase me around the wine shed even while your son was alive?"

She talked about it on purpose. It made her lips, her eyes, moist.

"Don't you like beef? . . . Have you come far?"

"Quite a bit, yes . . ."

"And you haven't got a sou left in your pocket. . . ."

He hunted through his pockets. As if in mockery, he found a sou.

"A sou, yes."

"We'll see. . . . First, we'll try and make the incubator work. I've wanted an incubator for a long time. Just think of it, the price chickens are now, you can hatch sixty-five all at once. The trouble is, it's secondhand, so I couldn't have the leaflet. There's a brass plate on top with things written on it."

She got up to get the coffeepot, and sipped her coffee, eyeing her guest all the while.

"Some of them at market this morning must have said: 'Tati's crazy! Now she's gone and bought herself an incubator.'"

She laughed. "Think how they'd chatter if. . . ."

Her eyes were eating him up. She was taking possession of

him. She wasn't afraid. She wanted him to understand that she wasn't afraid of him.

"A little drop of something? The old man won't get one and that'll make him mad...."

She brought a bottle of home brew, and poured out a few drops.

"And now, we'll try and make the thing work. Don't worry about the old man: it's time he went to look after his cows pasturing along the towpath.... Do you understand how it works?... I know you put the eggs in here, in this sort of drawer. And the lamp, I suppose, hooks into the corner. What's that written on the brass plate?"

Perhaps she didn't know how to read? It was quite possible. Or else the letters were too small.

"Raise the temperature to 102° and maintain it at that level for the 21 days of incubation...."

"How are we to know it's a hundred and two degrees?"

"There's a thermometer."

They were both squatting in front of the apparatus. The heat drenched their skin with sweat.

"Show me where the hundred-and-two-degree mark is."

"If we're going to try it, we'll need some kerosene."

"I've got some. Wait a minute...."

She got some from the shed. She cleaned the wick, lit the lamp.

"You're sure this is the place to put it?"

The big red bus had long since arrived at Montluçon, almost empty, having scattered its women all along the road. The driver was eating a snack in the shady dining room of a little restaurant, and he would start back at four o'clock.

From Montluçon to St. Amand, sometimes running

alongside the Cher, sometimes sweeping away from it, the Berry canal, barely twenty feet wide, bore toy boats on its calm waters, blocked here and there by toy bridges, little draw-bridges you had to work yourself by hauling on a chain.

It was the end of May. The gooseberries were ripe. The strawberries were beginning to fill out. In one corner of the garden there was a wide bed of beans.

"If they say you've got to put water in, water is what you've got to put in!"

Tati was suspicious. Jean groped around. Where was the proper place for the water that would keep the incubator moist?

He had taken off his jacket. His thin shirt, with its blue and white stripes, was worn at the collar and wrists.

He was thin, and yet there was a touch of puffiness in his face.

"We shall soon see," he said. "If the temperature reaches a hundred and two in a few minutes..."

"I've got some eggs all ready. All pure Leghorn. Where did you plan to spend the night?"

He smiled, which showed he had understood. Ever since the bus, before they had exchanged a word, they had understood one another.

"I don't know. Here, perhaps? Look! Ninety-nine...Almost a hundred...a few minutes now..."

"Would you sleep in the loft?"

"Why not?"

"And you would do what work there is to do?"

He took his stand in front of the yard swarming with poultry.

"So long as you're not afraid," he uttered, stretching nonchalantly.

"Afraid of what?"

"You don't know where I come from...."

"No man has ever scared me yet!"

"And yet, suppose..."

"Suppose what?"

"Well, suppose I'd just come out of prison?"

It was as if she had guessed it already.

"Well, what then?"

"Suppose I made off with your savings tonight?"

"You wouldn't find them."

"And suppose I murdered you?"

"I'm stronger than you are, my boy!"

"Suppose . . ."

"Suppose what?"

"Nothing . . ."

His playful mood had abated somewhat. He looked at her almost seriously. "You're an odd woman. Tell me, now. . . . The old man . . . didn't you say he was your father-in-law?"

"And you're surprised I mess around with him, eh? Well, first of all it's no fault of mine if he's an old tomcat. Then again, would you rather I let myself be thrown out of a house where I've done everything and let others benefit—pieces like that Félicie you saw?"

"Look! It's up to a hundred and two."

"Do you think it's working, then? If so, we'd better carry it into the wine shed. Wait . . . I'll give you a hand."

"Better wait till tomorrow to put the eggs in."

She agreed, but reluctantly. "That means a whole day lost."

Then, while they were settling the incubator in the cool shade of the wine shed: "It's up to you. As I said, I took you for a foreigner, a Polack or something. If you'd like a bed, your food, and a bit of money now and then. . . ."

Over the gate he could see the girl sitting on the canal embankment, her baby on her arm. She was feeding it at her breast. The bridge was raised. A boat was being poled imperceptibly forward. Farther off, on the other side of the water, he could see a brickyard. Pigeons flew heavily in the still air.

"Mind you, I don't want to force you. . . ."

Just then he gazed at the mole which looked like a bit of fur, at the broad face, the cunning eyes, the squat, solid body, the pink slip showing more than ever under the dress.

"We can always try," he said, "seeing you're not afraid. . . ."

Leading him back to the house like captured prey, she replied, "It'll take more than you to frighten me, my boy!"

There was no mistaking the familiarity of her tone. She had taken possession of him.

"Do you at least know how to use a crusher? Well, go and crush a sack of oats and wheat for the animals. . . . And you watch what a face Couderc pulls tonight!"

2

HIS BED, an iron one, set in the middle of the loft, just under the skylight, smelled of hay, with perhaps a hint of mustiness, which was by no means unpleasant. What puzzled him the whole of the time it took him to fall asleep were the drops falling one by one, at long intervals, inside the loft itself, almost within reach of his hand. Yet there was not a tap in the house. It was not raining, else he would have heard the drumming of the raindrops on the sloping glass of the skylight.

Abruptly, he switched from evening to morning and his only recollection of that night was of the smell, the smell of hay and mustiness, which became for him the smell of the countryside. The daylight cut out two bright rectangles above his head. In a corner of the loft stood a dressmaker's dummy, with its monstrous black torso, full yet without breasts, the geometric curve of the waist and those hips which came to a sudden stop, to be replaced by a leg in turned wood.

There was neither toilet nor basin, and he had to be content with pulling his trousers up over his shirttails, leaving the collar open, and smoothing his hair with his fingers.

The drops were still falling, from a kind of obscene udder suspended from one of the beams—a muslin bag containing white cheese. And on the floor was a bowl half full of a yellowish liquid.

All this, and other things besides, combined with the mattress to make up the smell: cloves of garlic, tied up with a scrap of bast, onions, shallots, and herbs that he didn't know—medicinal herbs, no doubt—so dry that they tumbled in a shower of dust as soon as they were barely touched.

He went down the staircase, which began by being no more than a miller's ladder and came out into the kitchen, where a few logs were blazing on the hearth. The stove was never lit first thing in the morning. Close to the ashes he saw a blue enamel coffeepot, with a big black star chipped off the enamel, and, as though already at home, he took a bowl from the cupboard, helped himself to coffee, hunted for the sugar, found it.

It was six o'clock in the morning. He saw nobody in the yard, but, hearing a noise in a shed, found Tati there busy scooping various ingredients out of bins and pouring them into a big cooking pot.

"Come and give us a hand!" she called out, already used to harrying him around.

Then, looking at his shoes, which he had not laced up: "There are some sabots in the washhouse. They're a pair of Couderc's sabots. Bring the hot water that's standing on the stove."

What with the dew and the poultry droppings, the ground was slippery and the fowls' prints formed a crisscross pattern upon it.

The sun was up, but there was still some haze in the air. A long trail of mist straggled between the two rows of trees along the canal. The old man was evidently milking the cows in the shed, for the milk could be heard squirting rhythmically into the pail; a heavy breath of animal warmth came from that direction, and from time to time a hoof banged against the partition.

"Try and remember the quantities. I've done all this by myself quite long enough! One pail of grits...one pail of bran...half a pail of fish meal...pour on the water now, slowly, just enough to make the bran curl."

There was a smell of bed and flannel about her. Over her

pink slip, which she must have slept in, she was wearing an old light brown coat that had lost both buttons and lining, and her hair was tied up in a kerchief. Her legs were naked, with blue veins showing.

"Now, fill the pails...."

She kept glancing at him covertly.

"I had a little girl from the orphanage to help me. I had to get rid of her, on account of that bastard of a Couderc. He used to take her into the shed to feel her, and it's a miracle things went no further. There ... come along."

And, while he carried the pails, she ladled the feed with a wooden scoop and filled the galvanized-iron troughs, onto which the chickens rushed.

"Next come the pigs."

He found livestock everywhere, in every corner, in every one of the outlandish buildings surrounding the yard: sitting hens; other hens sheltered, with their chicks, by a sort of trelliswork tent. And hutches piled one on top of the other, faced with wire netting, rabbits stirring inside.

When the three of them got back to the kitchen, Tati climbed on a chair and cut off three slices of ham, which she set on the frying pan. And so they ate, in silence, facing the window.

"Will you be able to go and cut some grass for the rabbits?"

"I think so."

She shrugged. That was no sort of an answer.

"Come along and I'll give you the sickle and a sack. You only have to cross the bridge. Between the canal and the Cher you'll find all the grass you want."

She called him back as he was moving off, with his crescent-shaped sickle held at arm's length.

"Try not to cut yourself...."

He still did not realize it was Sunday. It had not occurred to him. He was just a little surprised to see two barges moored above the lock, with hatches closed, as if the people inside were still asleep. Then he noticed a fisherman getting off his bicycle and settling down on the embankment.

The lock was a hundred yards or so from the house, and so narrow he could have jumped across. The shutters were still closed at the lock-keeper's cottage as well. The water of the canal seemed to be steaming gently, and now and again a bubble would rise to the surface.

Once across the bridge, he got a better idea of the lay of the land. Where the canal turned, a village appeared, or rather the beginnings of a village which would be about three quarters of a mile away. In front of him a meadow sloped steeply away to the Cher, whose clear water leapt over the pebbles, and immediately on the other side of the river there were thick woods.

The house where Félicie, the slut with the baby, lived was opposite the lock, between the canal and the Cher, and surrounded with heaps of pink bricks.

He bent down to cut the grass still wet with dew. An occasional bicycle passed along the towpath. He saw the hatchway of one of the barges being opened, and a woman not yet fully dressed came out to hang up washing on wires stretching from one end of the boat to the other.

A cow lowed. Old Couderc crossed the bridge behind his two beasts, their swollen udders heaving to the slow rhythm of their pace. As soon as they were on the grassy slope, they lowered their pink muzzles to the grass, while the old man, taking no notice, stood still, a stick in his hand.

Jean finally realized it was Sunday when he saw a whole troop of girls and boys bicycling by in their Sunday best, then a woman—doubtless the lock-keeper's wife—coming out of her cottage and making her way to the village, prayer book in hand.

He went up to the old man. "Well, now..." he said, as though the other had not been deaf.

And he winked at him, but Couderc, instead of responding

to this overture, turned his head away. He was probably wary, perhaps frightened, for when Jean came closer, he took two or three steps in the direction of his cows, as if to maintain the distance between them.

So, with his sack almost full of grass, Jean returned to the house.

Tati, all dressed up and wearing a hat, was putting a saucepan on the fire, which she had finally lit.

"I suppose you don't go to church?" she said without turning around.

There was a smell of onion being cooked. She took some cloves from the cupboard, and two bay leaves.

"Give the grass to the rabbits. Have a look at my stew now and then. If it sticks to the bottom, add a drop of water, but only a drop, and put the pot on the side of the stove."

A piece of mirror hung below a calendar. She looked at herself to straighten her hat, got her prayer book with its cover of black wool cloth. Then she turned to face him.

"You'll manage?" she asked.

And always that little glance in which he could read satisfaction, even a kind of promise, but a slight reservation as well. She was not distrustful. Only, she still needed to watch him for a time.

"I'll manage!"

"If you want to wash, just draw some water from the well. There's soap and a towel in the laundry."

Why were her eyes filling with sudden laughter?

"You haven't got a razor, I'll bet. For today, you can use the old man's. It must be in his room. I'll bring you one when I go to St. Amand."

A little while later, she was walking along the canal, short and solid, dressed in black from head to toe, clutching her prayer book to her bosom and holding an umbrella in her other hand.

He shaved in the kitchen, in front of the scrap of mirror, and then went to wash in the yard with the ice-cold water he drew from the well.

When he felt clean, with his chest bare under his open shirt, and his hair still damp, he wanted to smoke, but he had no cigarettes left. Nor had he the money to buy any.

By dint of prowling through the house, he managed to find a packet of rough-cut tobacco on the kitchen mantelpiece. Some pipes belonging to the old man were hanging in a rack. He chose one, and then, feeling a certain distaste for smoking a pipe Couderc had used before him, he went to the cupboard for the bottle of brandy, filled the bowl, and let the liquid trickle out through the stem.

From time to time he glanced at René, widow Couderc's son, stuck there in his frame, with cap, uniform, and the lopsided face of a degenerate.

"A little punk . . ." he growled.

He knew what he was talking about. A dirty little brute, and a liar in the bargain.

The stew was simmering, the meat was beginning to sizzle in the saucepan, and he did not forget, when he was afraid it might stick, to pour in a drop of water as he had been bidden.

After which he went outside, aimlessly, and reached the towpath, as free as air, like a man utterly without ties.

The old man was still with his cows across the water. The fisherman had rigged two bottom lines fitted with huge red floats, probably for carp or tench, and now he sat motionless on his campstool.

Cyclists were still passing, and some of them had bunches of lilac tied to the handlebars, people doubtless on their way to visit relatives in town. One of the bargees, standing up in his dinghy, was giving the side of his unladen barge a coat of resin, using a long-handled brush.

Jean reached the lock. The lock-keeper—he had a wooden leg—was sitting on his doorstep, mending an eel trap. The door was open. A baby was crying. And on the other side of the water the house in the brickyard had its door open too, but it was impossible to see what was going on inside.

He was about to turn back, because of the stew to be watched. His pipe was rather strong. Before, he used to smoke nothing but cigarettes. He turned around as he heard the bells of two bicycles. Two gendarmes were riding slowly along and looked closely at him.

The gendarmes rode on for another quarter of a mile or so. Then they got off and came back to him.

"Have you got your papers?"

Unlike the women in the bus, these two had made no mistake. Their thick eyebrows bristled with suspicion. They looked at each other with all the cunning of men you can't fool.

From his hip pocket Jean fetched out some folded papers which they inspected. From their pouches they took other papers, compared the two sets, moved away for a brief whispered discussion.

"You know you're not allowed to leave the Département?"

"I know."

"And that you must register as soon as you have a place to live?"

"I have one. I was meaning to come and report tomorrow."

There was a tinge of respect in the attitude of the two officers. If Jean had been an ordinary tramp, they would have spoken to him much more familiarly. But here was a man about whom special instructions had been sent, a man who had just done five years at Fontevrault.

"Where are you living?"

"At Madame Couderc's."

"She hired you?"

"As a farmhand."

"We're taking your papers along. You'll get them back when the inspector's seen them."

They mounted. Jean, hands in his pockets, jumped over the lock and prowled near the brickyard in the hope of seeing Félicie. He even glanced into the house. No doubt the little slut was at church, for all he could see, in the half darkness of the kitchen, where a bed had been set up, was the baby standing in a wicker frame which enabled it to walk. A woman noticed his presence and came to take a closer look. She looked crabby, had an evil eye. Finding nothing to say to him, she banged the door in his face, even if that left her in almost total darkness.

So, at loose ends, he went and sat down beside the fisherman, who made no effort to engage in conversation and kept on placidly throwing into the water the little pellets smelling of cheese that he used as bait.

Sitting there, he saw Tati come back from church. A little later he noted the two gendarmes, who were riding just as slowly as before along the towpath. They got off their bicycles outside the house and went into the kitchen.

They came out again a good quarter of an hour later, wiping their mustaches, which showed they had been given a drink.

Tati had not changed her dress. The cameo on her bosom produced almost the same effect as the downy mole on her left cheek. She had stacked the dirty dishes in a pail, wiped the table, and then suggested, "We might go and sit outside. Put the armchair and another chair in front of the door...."

He realized that this was part of the traditional Sunday ritual. The armchair was made of wickerwork, with a red seat cushion and a triangular cushion as a headrest. For all her Sunday best, Tati went and took off her shoes, which probably pinched, and came back in a brand-new pair of blue slippers.

"In a little while, we'll put the eggs in the incubator. This morning it was a hundred and one. If we turn up the wick a little more...."

But it was Sunday. She was in no hurry. The gendarmes had had their drop of brandy, as two unwashed little glasses bore witness.

"You took one of Couderc's pipes?"

By the way, where was the old man? He had disappeared immediately after the meal.

"I haven't any cigarettes left," Jean admitted.

"I'll give you three francs to go and buy some. But don't you go and spend all afternoon in the village!"

And, as she watched him go, she spread some knitting on her lap and picked up her needles.

The village was almost empty. Two boys of sixteen or seventeen, their faces scrubbed shiny, shouted as they tried to amuse themselves.

On the way back, Jean met old Couderc, who had put on his Sunday clothes at last and, in his black suit and broad white tie, looked as if he were going to a wedding or a funeral. He was walking along the canal, his pace slack. He did not see, or pretended not to see, his new lodger.

"You didn't stay too long. That's good. That's good! Sit down. Take a chair with a back."

He brought a chair from the kitchen, one with a straw seat, and settled himself astride it. Then, without speaking, he puffed out the blue smoke of his cigarette, and watched a little boy who was fishing with a stick he had cut in the woods.

Tati knitted on. Her needles made a clicking sound and now and then, when she counted her stitches, her lips could be seen moving. Whenever she turned her head, he knew it was to peer at him.

When, after a very long time, she finally made up her mind to speak, it was to say, "There's not a man living that can frighten me."

Then, as if in anger, "You're all alike! You show off. You look as if you wanted to smash everything, when really..."

He did not answer. Perhaps he had become a little more grave? A shadow had passed. He could no longer see the little boy fishing.

"The gendarmes said to me: 'From now on, it's up to you! You can't say you haven't been warned....'"

Another silence, another row of knitting.

"And *I* said to them: 'Don't you worry! He won't try to put anything over on *me....*'"

"Did they tell you my name?"

"Passerat-Monnoyeur. An easy name to remember, seeing it's on all the bottles. Funny, your having the same name as the distiller at Montluçon."

"It isn't funny."

"What do you mean?"

"It isn't funny, he's my father."

He shot it out lightly, as though for his own amusement, and in the same key she replied, "That's enough!"

"What's enough?"

"Look, son...I know Monsieur Passerat-Monnoyeur. And well I should know him, seeing my sister was in service there for years. He's far too proud a man to let his son go to prison. Besides, he's so rich that his son would have no need to...."

She stopped, looked him in the eye, asked, "Perhaps you don't like talking about it?"

"Well..."

"All right! Not that I care to. The gendarmes told me the whole story. They warned me I was keeping you at my own risk. So, now, it's my turn to warn you. Do you understand, my boy?... I'm not afraid of you, or anybody. Today is Sunday, and we can rest a bit...."

She noticed that her tone was less familiar, perhaps because they had been talking of the Passerat-Monnoyeurs.

"But you'd better toe the line, understand? And you'll have to get up earlier in the morning, because livestock won't wait to be fed until the sun's halfway up the sky. Go and get my glasses. On the mantelpiece, on the right..."

Toward three o'clock there were quite a few people strolling along the canal. Some came from the village, walking leisurely, in family groups, the children walking in front and kicking at the stones. Most of all, there were people on bicycles and a few tourists with packs on their backs. The grass was a dark green, the water almost black. In contrast, the newborn foliage of the chestnuts was tender and the sunshine splashed it with large daubs of gold.

"How long have you been out?"

"Five days."

"René only did six months and I used to go and see him every week. Poor kid! And what for? A few lighters they couldn't have sold without getting themselves pinched, some receipt stamps and some pipes..."

"They broke into a tobacco shop?"

"There was a gang, four or five of them. They'd been drinking. It happened in St. Amand. The shop had no shutters and at night you could see all the things in the window. They smashed the glass. When he got home, I didn't suspect anything. I simply noticed he'd been sick. Next morning he went to work as usual. He was learning carpentry at St. Amand.

"The police and the gendarmes looked for six weeks and if that fool Chagot...

"Unhealthy young devil, and vicious like nobody's business...He started talking in his sleep, at night. His father works in a hardware store. The sort of people who think themselves more respectable than other folks.

"The idiot—Chagot's father, I mean—went off to the police, stiff as a ramrod, with tears in his voice, and his big hands shook. 'My duty as a citizen and a father...' he told them. And the whole story. The youngster was pulled in. They didn't have to question him for long. He still had a stolen lighter in his pocket. 'It was Couderc's idea...' Which just wasn't true: my son never could have such a notion.

"Now he's over there, in Africa. I send him money every week. He writes me long letters. One day I'll read them to you...."

Why was her tone still formal? Jean went on smoking cigarettes, his arms resting on the back of his chair, looking at nothing in particular. A whole family had settled down on the grass not far from them, and the mother was cutting up a pie she had just taken out of its newspaper wrapping.

"It must be long, five years, eh?"

The sun had just reached them. All at once, their skins had begun to take on their summer smell.

"And all that time, no women?"

He shrugged.

"And since?"

He smiled, shook his head. She sighed.

"It's probably time we went and put the eggs in the incubator. In the country Sunday never lasts all day."

They set out the eggs one by one, after candling them. The lamp was refilled with kerosene, the wick cleaned, water poured into the container designed to keep the whole contrivance moist. All that time, it was clear that Tati was thinking of nothing else.

"There's a woman near Orléans who ships out three-day-old

chicks, in specially made cardboard boxes, and sells them at five francs each. Sixty times five francs every month, allowing for breakage . . ."

And the next minute: "You'd better put on your jacket. It's going to get cooler. Next week, I'll buy you some things. That's no fit suit for country work. Tell me!"

"What?"

"Why did you lie just now, when I mentioned the distiller? Why did you tell me he was your father? Trying to be clever, eh?"

"I don't know."

"You're as stupid as René. . . . Here! Fill this bucket with oats. Every evening, at this time, it's your job to scatter barley for the chickens. Then you go and get grass for the rabbits against the next day. That way, you've got time for other things in the morning."

The day had flowed away like water, and it was a surprise to see the patches of sunlight grow red while the sky turned purple.

"Is it true, what you told me just now? That since you came out you haven't. . . ."

The fire had died out in the kitchen. Only a few logs would be lit to warm up the evening soup.

"This being the first Sunday, we can treat ourselves to a nip of something. Couderc is at the café, playing cards as usual. I often wonder how he manages to play, deaf as he is. To think that, till he turned fifty, he was a man like any other. It began with me, even while Marcel was still alive. Marcel was my husband. His health was poor. The old man was always after me. . . . Drink up! It's a five-year-old brandy, distilled here, from wine made with the grapes of the vine that's behind the house."

Sunrays as sharp as the beams from a searchlight slanted in through the window with its small panes. Tati was still holding her glass and did not know which way to look.

"Maybe there's a suit upstairs that would fit you. Anyway, I must go and take off my good dress."

She wondered whether to pour him another drink, decided it was not necessary. "Come and see."

Her room was clean, with whitewashed walls, furnished with a great mahogany bed and an ancient cupboard. She opened it, releasing whiffs of mothball.

"Here. Try on this pair of trousers. They belong to Marcel. Meanwhile, I'll be changing. . . ."

The blind was down, allowing only a golden light to filter through. The eider down on the bed was blood-red.

"Feeling shy? . . . Your skin's as white as a girl's."

Then she laughed, a harsh little laugh, as she looked pointedly at a particular part of his body. "Have you forgotten how?"

What followed brought back to Jean old memories of his teens, of a night when he and a friend, the son of a building contractor, had pooled their pocket money and furtively made their way into a well-known establishment of Montluçon.

The same coarse words. The same crude gestures. And that very same domination by the woman who left him no initiative, for whom he was only an object. The same candid obscenity.

"Glad?"

He would have astonished her by revealing that the whole time he had looked at nothing but her hairy mole, had thought of nothing but that bit of fur adorning her face.

"Only, I give you fair warning: don't try to take advantage. I've got a mind of my own! It's all right to have our fun now and then. . . ."

She was putting on her pink flannel slip, her old dress.

"But work is still work. What are you doing?"

He had raised the blind, and was looking through the window at the towpath where the local people came for a stroll.

"You'd better look for a pair of trousers to fit you. As for Couderc, he can just go and chase himself tonight. Aren't you ready yet?"

A little boy was fishing and once in a while pulled up a tiny fish from the water. A young man and a girl were walking side by side, heads down, not touching one another. Perhaps they had just had an argument? Or were they still only on the brink of whispering the words they hesitated to speak? Perhaps they were gambling their whole lives, there, in the sunset, while the shadows of the trees lengthened out of all proportion.

She had a yellow flower in her hand and was beating the air with it as with a whip. His arms were too long, and he did not know what to do with them.

A two-year-old nearly bumped into them, and his mother, who sat on the embankment beside her husband, called, "Henri! . . . Henri! . . . Come here this minute!"

The gendarmes rode by, slowly, gravely, for the third time that day, on bicycles as heavy as themselves.

"Time to go and lock up the chickens," said Tati, opening the door. Then, looking at him suspiciously: "Anyone would say you hadn't liked it!"

He smiled—a nice, polite smile. "I did."

"Well, then, hurry up. I'm going to put the soup on."

Was she pleased with him? Displeased? She didn't know yet. As she left the room, she glanced once more at the bedroom and the cupboard in front of which he was trying on a pair of her late husband's trousers.

3

TATI, WHO was never still the whole day long and, as she hurried to and fro, seemed to carry the entire household on her robust shoulders, had her hour of weakness.

It was after the midday meal, which they called dinner. The later in the season, the more striking was the contrast between the out of doors white with sun and the cool shade of the kitchen. In particular, deep in a recess that looked like a niche and had probably been made by removing the doors of a closet, there always stood two buckets of water drawn from the well, a big mug beside them, and never, not even at a spring deep in the woods, had Jean had so strong an impression of limpidity, so keen a desire to feel the cold water run down his throat.

The door from the yard was kept shut, because of the flies, and also to stop the poultry from invading the kitchen. But underneath there was still a broad gap, a band of molten gold in which the chicken's feet could be seen in restless movement.

His last mouthful swallowed, Couderc would wipe his knife on the table, which was deeply notched at the place where he sat. Then, like a beast placing itself between the shafts, he would unwind his long, thin body and lumber off to some corner of the yard, where he was soon to be heard shifting boxes or barrels around.

He would putter about, mending fences, trimming gateposts, splitting logs for the fire, or again sorting out pea sticks or props for tomatoes, his eye glassy, a drop on the end of his nose always, winter or summer.

Then, with a shove of her stomach against the still-uncleared table, Tati would push back her chair, its straw bottom groaning as she did so. A sigh would issue from her vast bosom, and her breasts at this hour always seemed to nestle cozily on her swollen belly; her skin was shiny, her eye moist.

Jean had already fallen into the habit of getting the coffee from the fire, and the blue coffeepot had its place right in a sunbeam falling from the window.

Tati would contemplate her glass—she always had her coffee in a glass. The two lumps of sugar would dissolve. She would watch them almost sentimentally, then sip a drop or two of the brown liquid.

It was as though, for miles around, life hung suspended. The bargees on the canal were napping, while the donkeys or mules rested in a patch of shade. There was not a sound to be heard except the cooing of the pigeons, drowned now and then by the crowing of a cock or the banging of the old man's hammer.

"To think that, when I first came to this house, at fourteen, I came as a servant girl."

Tati's gaze caressed the walls: they had not changed, they had just had a fresh coat of whitewash each year. The combined calendar and newspaper holder, with its oleograph picture of reapers, must be the one that had been there all that time ago. On either side of the ancient kneading trough, used now for keeping odds and ends, two portraits in oval frames had not changed either.

"That's Couderc as he was then."

The same elongated head, with its wiry hair cropped short. A pointed mustache slashing the face. The hard look of someone well aware of his own importance.

"He was thirty-five then! He owned the brickyard, inherited

it from his father. He was born in this house. The land reached as far as the village, and there were ten cows in the cowshed."

She stirred the spoon around in her glass, and lapped another sip of coffee, with all the luxurious greed of a cat.

"His wife had just died, and he was left alone with three children. When I came, they had just buried her, and the house still smelled of candles and chrysanthemums."

The other portrait, which made a pair with Couderc's, had faded more quickly, as if realizing it was no more than the shade of a dead woman. The features were hazy, indistinct. A sad smile. A high chignon. A cameo, the one Tati wore on Sundays.

"I don't know how my mother had heard they were looking for someone to care for the children. We lived far from here, near Bourges. A neighbor drove me over in his gig. For fear they might think I was too young, my mother had put my hair up and made me wear a long dress."

Sometimes there were harsh notes in her voice, like pebbles.

"The boy was eleven and nearly as tall as I was. The two sisters were called Françoise and Amélie. They were stupid and dirty, especially Françoise. You've seen her. She's Félicie's mother. She married Tordeux, who's barely fit to be watchman at a brickyard."

Jean was relaxing too, still astride a chair, his elbows on its back, a slender thread of smoke rising from his cigarette.

And Tati sighed: "That's the whole story!"

She knew how she meant it. For her the walls, everything in the room, became alive. She could see them again at different periods—when, for instance, just fourteen years old, she was the first of the household to get up and, in the depth of winter, light the fire in the cold kitchen, before going to break the ice in the horse trough.

"Couderc was on the town council. He could have got himself elected mayor. He was a serious sort of man then, who wouldn't so much as look twice at a woman. I've never known how he came to start losing money. Some sort of partnership with a contractor who went bankrupt, and that made him sell the brickyard."

Jean would have liked to see a portrait of Tati as a young girl. Had she even then had that air of authority, that way of looking people over as though reckoning just how far you could go with them?

She always looked at him in that fashion, as she had done on that first morning in the bus. She had grown used to him. She had held him naked in her arms, she had stroked his white skin. At dawn she would sometimes climb up to the loft and, before waking him, watch him for a moment as he slept.

But for all that she still spied on him, still kept him on the end of a string.

"I was seventeen when the boy, who wasn't much cleverer than his sisters, got me in the family way. I can still remember exactly how it happened. He was in bed with a sore throat. I had taken some broth up to him.

"'You got a fever,' I said. And he said to me—he must have been rehearsing it for hours to get his courage up: 'Look!... This is why I've got a fever!'

"Couderc was furious, but finally got us married. The daughters married too. Françoise married the watchman at the brickyard and the other one, Amélie, married a clerk from St. Amand."

"Any coffee left?"

She looked at the time. The pendulum swung its shining disk from left to right and right to left behind the glass of the clock case.

She allowed herself a few minutes more.

"One day you'll have to tell me what you did."

She looked at him more intently.

"Did you kill for a woman? All right! I'm not asking questions. I can see how it'd bother you."

Come! It was time to get up, to shake off the warm numbness penetrating their every limb. She made sure there was not a drop of coffee left in the blue coffeepot, brought the kettle from the stove, poured the hot water into the dishpan, dropped in a handful of flakes.

"This afternoon you'd better go and hoe the potatoes. Any moment now I guess the old man will turn up. He's been hot and bothered for two or three days now, and if I don't let him have his way...."

And so he got to know the story of the Coudercs. He would learn a bit here and a bit there, and piece the bits together. Tati's husband alone he could not picture, and he had not been shown a single portrait of him. Perhaps there wasn't one in the house?

A man in poor health. And sad, so far as he could judge. He had died of pneumonia. While he was still alive, old Couderc had already made a habit of pursuing his daughter-in-law in the darkness of the outbuildings.

"You see," said Tati another time during her after-dinner hour, "it isn't Françoise I'm afraid of. She's too stupid. Even when she was a child they made fun of her because she never took anything in. A boy made her believe that children are made with the nose, and she cried and cried over it. As for Amélie, I can stand up to her. The real pest is that slut of a Félicie who's always hanging around her grandfather and showing him her baby. She's a different breed, she is, and I'd be curious to know who fathered her. Not Françoise's husband, for sure. One look at her is enough to prove that."

Jean saw her often from afar. Perhaps it was this very remoteness that impressed him so much?

Because of the canal embankment, all that could be seen of the house was the pink-tiled roof and the upper part of the white wall. It was Félicie's custom, as day began to decline and the sun was setting behind her, to take up position near the lock, her baby on her arm.

She was thin. She bent under the weight like the stalk of a too heavy flower. She would have seemed a mere child if the movement she made to support the baby had not thrown out her stomach, which gave her a mature and womanly look.

The blue of her smock and the red of her hair stood out from a long way off.

Jean would amble along the towpath and come nearer. He knew she watched his approach. He knew that under her greenish eyes there were golden freckles, and also that the watching made her screw up her nose.

So as not to startle her, he would exaggerate his nonchalance, stopping to watch an angler's cork or to pick a yellow flower from the bank.

The wooden-legged lock-keeper turned his cranks. His children were sitting on the doorstep and an armless doll lay on the gravel.

Jean would move a few yards nearer, and invariably Félicie would suddenly turn her back and hurry to her house, shutting the door behind her.

He was the enemy, no doubt of that. Once, as he moved nearer still, the door opened again, but it was not Félicie who appeared. It was her mother, Françoise, stupid and surly, who took up her stand in the doorway in defense of her lair.

"How's things?" he would ask the lock-keeper mechanically.

And the lock-keeper would dart a suspicious look at him, and turn his back too.

Jean was unconcerned. In his eyes, there remained the same lightness of expression. Was he thinking? Did he still need to think?

He was living uncovenanted hours, hours he had not reckoned on, and his head was full of light, his nostrils drunk with summer scents, his limbs heavy with peace.

"Jean!...Jean!..." called Tati's shrill voice.

She was there in front of her house, fists on hips, short of leg, short of neck, strong of flesh.

"Prowling around Félicie again, eh? Hurry up and clean out the rabbit hutches. I've been telling you that for three days now. If I've got to do everything myself, it's not worth my...."

Twice, three times a day the two of them would lean over the incubator, which for Tati was truly a magic box. She did not yet dare believe that sixty chickens would hatch out at once.

"Read out again what it says. I haven't got my glasses. You're sure we don't have to put more water in? At night I'm always frightened the lamp will go out and I don't know what stops me from taking a look. On Saturday I'll bring you back a razor and everything you need. By then I hope I'll get a letter from René."

She had visitors first. On Thursday. The after-dinner slack was just over and she had begun the dishes.

"I want you to clear the weeds along the side of the house," she had said to Jean.

For all along the white wall nettles had grown. He had brought a hoe from the shed. Hatless, his shirt open, a cigarette between his lips, he was beginning to hoe the ground when he heard noises at the end of the hollow path.

A hundred yards away, shaded by the hazels which let through only a few roundels of sun, a family group was approaching—a man in dark clothes with a little beard and a straw hat, a rather stout woman who probably perspired from walking, and a little boy in a sailor suit whom she was dragging along by the hand and who was whipping the air with a switch he had cut.

In peasant fashion, Jean stood still, watching their approach as though it were an interesting show. He noted that the family paused for a brief consultation. The woman took the opportunity to tug at her girdle, and then, her son having bent down to pick something up, she gave his hand a shake.

"What is it, Jean?" Tati called from the kitchen, seeing him stock-still.

He did not catch the words, for both door and window were shut. He merely saw the movement of her lips, and he opened the window a bit.

"Visitors, I think."

Frowning, already beginning to tidy her hair, she came and leaned out.

"It's Amélie and her husband. I'm going to clean up a little. Tell them I'll be down in a minute."

In a flash she had whisked the dishes into the cupboard and gone upstairs, where she could be heard walking busily about.

The others, who had covered another fifty yards, paused again on seeing Jean in front of the door, hoe in hand. Another consultation. The husband wore eyeglasses and there was a purple ribbon in the buttonhole of his lapel.

They finally stepped forward, having come to a decision. They marched past the young man as though he had not existed and Amélie pushed the door half open.

"Are you there, Tati?" she called into the emptiness of the house.

"If you wish to go in, Tati will be down in a minute."

The woman drew back as if to avoid any contact with him. Her husband actually made a detour around Jean so as not to brush against him, and ordered his son: "Go ahead. Sit down on a chair and try to keep still."

Just because they were pretending to ignore him, Jean went in too, leaving his hoe outside, and drew up chairs for them.

"Sit down. It's warm out, isn't it? I suppose you didn't walk all the way from St. Amand?"

The husband let slip involuntarily, "We took the bus."

And his wife gave him a look of thunder for speaking to this individual.

Silence. She had sat down. The husband remained standing,

mopping his brow, taking off his hat to run a handkerchief over his bald head.

"Sit still, Hector."

Overhead, the heavy tread of Tati, who was hurriedly putting on her good dress and combing her hair.

Addressing her husband and still ignoring Jean, Amélie said, to break the silence, "I'm sure Father is out minding the cows. One of these days, with a sun like this, he'll have a stroke."

At length Tati started downstairs, opened the door, and came toward her sister-in-law.

"Good afternoon, Amélie."

Two kisses, one on each cheek, hard and dry as the peck of a bird.

"I didn't think you'd be coming today. Your husband has a day off? Good afternoon, Désiré. Go ahead and sit down! Good afternoon, Hector. Won't you say good afternoon to your aunt?"

"Good afternoon, Aunt. I'd like to go fishing in the canal."

"I forbid you to go fishing!" cried his mother. "I've no wish to see you fall in the water. Stay here."

Jean was ready to leave at a look or a sign from Tati. It was she who kept him back.

"Get the bottle of brandy, Jean. You'll find some blackcurrant syrup for Amélie just inside the cellar door."

She brought some gold-rimmed glasses from the sideboard in the dining room.

"Well, what's the good news?" she asked, sitting down with a sigh of satisfaction. "You can stay, Jean. We have no secrets. Have we, Amélie? Is Désiré pleased with his new job? Is he still at the drugstore on the Rue Gambetta?"

"Still there!" was the tart reply.

"That's fine! Here's to you. Can the youngster have a drop of black currant?"

"Thanks! I would rather he didn't drink."

"I'm thirsty, Mamma."

"You'll get a glass of water. Father not here?"

"He must be somewhere about with the cattle."

"How is he?"

"Same as ever."

And then the declaration of war suddenly came.

"We had a letter from Françoise yesterday."

"Well, my poor dear, if it's Françoise who wrote it, you can't have gathered much. She's never been able to write in her life and all she can read is large-sized print."

"Félicie wrote it for her."

"Is she in the family way again? Of course, what with all these boats passing and the bargees wanting their bit of fun . . ."

Jean stood with his back against the wall, arms folded, not bothering to light his cigarette that had gone out.

"At least," Amélie struck back, "the gendarmes have never had to set foot in her house."

"Why do you say that? You had a visit from the gendarmes?"

"Somebody has. Anyway, Françoise is coming. I'm surprised she's not here already."

"What time did you fix?"

Unthinkingly, Amélie said:

"Three o'clock."

It was ten to. Perhaps just to keep things going, Désiré reached out for his glass. His wife stopped him.

"I'd rather you didn't drink. You know it upsets you."

"Well, my friends, we'll wait for Françoise. It's a good long time since I've seen her in this house. Of course, she does send her daughter over when I'm out to scrounge some ham or some eggs. Why only last Saturday——"

"Félicie has every right to come and see her grandfather."

"She could ask my leave before taking my ham."

"It's just as much Father's ham as yours. Everything here belongs to him, and therefore belongs to the family. That's the first of the things I meant to tell you."

"Why? Have you come to fetch something?"

"Wait till Françoise gets here," hissed her husband, fidgeting on his chair.

They saw Françoise go by the window. She hesitated a good minute or two before knocking at the door. She too was dressed up in her best. She had big timorous eyes, and she did not know what to do with her hands.

"Good afternoon, Amélie. Good afternoon, Désiré. Good afternoon, Hector. Am I late? I was frightened of getting here before you did, because, what with all the goings on here...."

A deep sigh.

"Sit down, Françoise," said Amélie. "Is your husband keeping well?"

"He hasn't had an attack for more than a month now."

"And the brickyard?"

"Going from bad to worse. One of these days it'll be put up for sale and I wonder whether the new owners would keep us on. Then we shall be out on the street. It's hard to think we have a house, and...."

Her eyes traveled around the walls, and then she heaved another sigh.

"We were just telling Tati you had written to us...."

That frightened poor Françoise. Undoubtedly she would have liked not to be brought directly into the affair.

"You haven't seen Father?"

"He doesn't even dare come near us. You can tell he's terrified, the poor man."

And Amélie said, after a meaningful glance at the corner where Jean was standing, "That's easily understood."

Désiré swallowed hard and boldly ventured, "When one must live night and day with people fresh from prison...."

And Tati, with deep satisfaction: "Especially when he ought to be there himself! Do you remember poor little Juliette? A kid of fourteen and an orphan. She was still of an age to play with dolls, and the poor little thing didn't dare say a word, she was so frightened."

"It's not for you to judge Father's actions. You know very well that, since his accident, he's not been the same as other people."

"Especially when he was so much better than others before!"

"Be quiet, Tati. I forbid you, a stranger, to——"

"What will you forbid me to do? To tell the truth? To say that your father is an old bastard, and that, no later than last week, he exposed himself in front of a little girl on her way home from school? Why, Françoise knows her! She can ask her if it isn't true. It's Cotelle's daughter, of the Moulin Neuf. . . ."

"Just the same," shrilled Amélie, "the house is his! And you're in his home, and you dare bring under his roof people that have no right to hold up their heads. Go and get Father, Françoise. Hector, you go and sit on the doorstep, but don't you dare go play beside the canal, or else you get a hiding. . . . Do you hear? Go on out."

"I don't want to go out. I'm thirsty."

"Have a drink of water."

"Désiré, will you or will you not make that child go outside?"

A smack rang out. Françoise had gone, heavy and stupid, swollen with anger and fear.

"We'll soon see whether we shall have to take steps!" declared Amélie, who was decidedly the brains of the family. "I may as well tell you right now that I've been to see a lawyer."

"To get Couderc thrown in jail?"

"Stop trying to be funny. You know you've got the short end of the stick. We know you, my girl! We know your brazen ways, and that ever since you stepped into the house you've wanted to run things your own way. My poor brother—rest his soul—could vouch for that."

"Pour me out another drink, will you, Jean? Why don't you sit down? I'd warned you it was an odd family, hadn't I?"

"Aren't you ashamed?"

"What of?"

"Having a murderer in the house. True, your son's not much better. If Mamma should see us! Our poor Mamma! She who . . ."

She looked at the faded portrait. Her eyes grew moist.

"A good thing she's dead, for now she would die of shame and grief."

Françoise's voice was heard on the path. She must be talking for the sake of talking, possibly to reassure herself, for the old man following her, with his head lowered as if she had him at the end of a halter, was incapable of hearing a word.

"Come in, poor Father."

Dazzled by the sun outside, he was blinking in the effort to make out the faces in the half darkness of the kitchen.

"Sit down. Have you got the note, Désiré? As for you, Tati, we'll soon see what Father thinks of all your scheming. Where was he, Françoise? Full in the sun, eh? To think that at his age he has to do all the heavy work. He's being treated like a worthless old workhorse till he breaks under the strain. Show him the note, Désiré."

As it was impossible to speak to the old man, they had written to him. Désiré, a cautious man, had taken care to make the letters large and blocked.

The family have decided that you should come and live in our house. You cannot go on working like a horse. You will be well cared for and you won't have to live with murderers anymore.

He kept looking at the piece of paper stupidly, wondering

what was wanted of him. He was by no means reassured. And oddly enough it was Tati that he clung to.

"You don't even know, the whole lot of you, that the old fool can't read any more without glasses! And the joke would be on you if I didn't give them to him. But I want him to read your piece of paper. Poor old devil! If I wasn't by, he couldn't even button up his fly...."

She went to a drawer, got out a pair of steel-rimmed spectacles, and put them on Couderc's nose. He still hesitated to read, as though he scented a trap.

He had several tries at it. Perhaps the lenses were not strong enough?

"Here, you old goat! You're entitled to a drink too."

She gave them a defiant look.

"If you think I don't see through your little game! It isn't the old man you're after! He'd be a nuisance to you! You wouldn't keep him a week without having him shut up in an asylum. And that's the truth! You needn't glower like that, Amélie. I know all about you! It's not my fault you married a man who earns seven hundred francs a month and has to change jobs every year because he always thinks he knows better than the boss. As for you, my poor Françoise, you're so stupid that, instead of speaking to you, one always wants to hold out a handful of hay. Well! What does your father say? Look at him! Try and get him to go with you!"

He was in terror. A child being kidnapped in a park could not have looked back with more anguish than did the old man as he turned toward Tati.

Yet Amélie was smiling at him for all she was worth, smiling and clucking as one does when trying to gain the confidence of an animal new to the house.

"Write to him that he'll be well cared for, Désiré, and that he'll have nothing to do but stroll all day long. And write too that there's a murderer in the house and that one fine day he might get it."

Then, turning to Tati: "You see, I know what you're up to. It's no accident that this man's here. One fine morning you'll get Father—God knows how—to sign a paper. Then he'll have to be disposed of before he can change his mind. Go on, admit it! Admit that from the first day you stepped in here, when we were still only kids, you decided *you* would take over. Our poor brother was properly fooled. You were already as perverted as could be. And I sometimes wonder if that isn't what he died of. Have you finished writing, Désiré?"

He handed her a little black notebook in which he had written a few lines.

"Write too that he's in danger of his life here."

Old Couderc would have liked to go. He had emptied his glass, and Amélie sighed: "On top of it all she gives him brandy, knowing full well he could never stand it and that the doctor forbids."

"Read it, Couderc," snapped Tati, who, seeming vastly amused, had planted herself in the middle of the kitchen, her hands on her hips. "You'll be happy with them all right, in three rooms on the first floor of a miserable gray house. And who'll there be to make love to you, eh?"

"Tati!" exclaimed Amélie, leaping to her feet.

"As if you didn't know! As if you didn't know it began while your brother was still alive! Look at him now, all of you. D'you think he wants to go off with you?"

He had risen, and had let the notebook fall to the floor. He had gone to sit by the chimney, to be as far out of reach as he could.

"You're taking advantage of him not being all there. But you haven't won the game for all that, Tati, I warn you. In cases like this, there is always the right to have a family council named. I know what the lawyer told me. And when that happens..."

She looked at the walls around her, made a sweeping gesture. "You'll be thrown out of here with your murderer."

She was quivering, her lips trembling. The sun-drenched window caught her eye. It doubtless reminded her of something, for she cried, "Where's Hector? Désiré! Quick—go and find Hector. He might have . . ."

Tati was smiling, a broad, beaming smile, and her hand was fiddling with the cameo pinned to the black silk bodice of her dress, the cameo her mother-in-law wore in the portrait.

"You really won't take anything to calm you down?" she asked, grasping the bottle of black-currant syrup.

Then, suddenly, Amélie did a foolish thing. She grabbed the bottle, which shattered on the floor. Tati's automatic response was to snatch off her hat, which fell into the red and sticky puddle.

"Amélie! . . . Tati! . . ." yelped Françoise, crazy with fear.

"It's lucky I can control myself," panted Amélie while she looked fearfully at Jean in case he might intervene. "Where's Désiré? Désiré! . . . Désiré! . . . Hector! . . . Where are you both?"

She had opened the door. The sun, coming into the kitchen, painted on the red tiles a broad lozenge dancing with fine dust.

Amélie wanted to cry. Françoise had got up.

"Désiré! . . . Hector! . . . I'll bet that child's gone and fallen into the canal. . . ."

This gave her an excuse for sobbing.

"You go too, old girl!" Tati advised as she gently pushed the inert Françoise before her. "Go and find your slut of a daughter. Go on! . . ."

And she kicked the door to.

"It's the house. . . ." she declared, coming back to the middle of the room and addressing Jean. "They get positively sick at the thought that they won't have the house to share between themselves. But who's got to put up with the old man, I ask you? Would it be fair?"

For the first time, she was looking at Couderc with a sort of tenderness.

"The idea of losing his Tati and not having his bit of fun now and then...!"

She stroked his cheek, and narrowed her eyes in a look of promise. "Come on! *This* time you'll have really earned it."

She jerked her head in the direction of the staircase. Jean had his back to her just then, but he had the impression that she made an obscene gesture.

He was looking out the window. Amélie, hatless, her hair disheveled, was delivering a violent harangue, to the shame of her husband. The child, one shoe dripping with water, had evidently just been slapped, for one of his cheeks was red and he was rubbing his eyes with his dirty hands.

Amélie and Françoise embraced, the way people do after a funeral.

Then the three from St. Amand made off toward the main road where they would have a wait of an hour and a half for the bus.

When Jean turned around, there was no one left in the kitchen. He could hear noises overhead and he preferred to go out into the yard where the chickens huddled in the shade of the cart.

What was there to be done that day?

He turned the well wheel and began watering the lettuces.

4

THAT SATURDAY turned out like one of those special days which a child anticipates for too long.

Did it not indeed begin with childish impressions? Jean's panic when, half awake, he heard the drumming of the rain on the sloping glass just over his head! On all the other days the weather had been radiant. Was it going to rain on purpose? He had to make an effort to open his eyes halfway. He had always been a heavy sleeper, coming to only with difficulty. It was still dark, fortunately. What time could it be? There was a moon, and the drops of water glistened as they slid down their zigzag track.

He went to sleep again, telling himself that the weather could still improve, and when he heard a door bang and leapt to his feet, the sun was indeed shining bravely, a richer, graver sun than on other mornings, and the chestnut trees were a deeper green.

When he was in the shed, getting the mash ready for the poultry, Tati's window opened. Tati leaned out, busy combing her hair as it hung down on her shoulders.

"Don't forget the pullets in the basket!"

And he felt as light as air, light as one is when something out of the ordinary is sure to happen. He whistled as he carefully arranged all the things Tati was to take to market: a basket of white pullets, tied in pairs by the feet; twelve dozen hen's eggs; three dozen duck's eggs (for the pastry cook) and five big goose's eggs; then the bricks of butter wrapped in cabbage leaves.

"Did you pick the red currants?" she called to him again, almost ready by now.

The old man was busy with his cows. The kitchen garden was damp. Tati did not want to waste anything, and, there being a gardenful of red currants, she was taking them off to market.

She snatched a bite, without sitting down, for she was always afraid of missing her bus.

"Hurry up, Jean! Mind the eggs!"

She frowned. Perhaps she found him too lively? He was still whistling as he loaded himself with the biggest baskets, and he strode out along the sunken path where the ground, after the rain, was a richer brown and the bushes gave off a heavy scent.

"If she comes to the house, don't be afraid to throw her out. Oh! I nearly forgot . . . the insurance man might call. He always picks a Saturday. The money's in the tureen in the dining room. It's the right amount."

For the first time, he saw again the small blue-fenced house beside the main road, and this time its door was half open.

"Good-bye, Clémence!" Tati called, though she could see nobody.

Someone moved inside. A woman who was cleaning herself up stuck her head out of the window and called in the same fashion, "Good-bye, Tati."

Then they waited, looking in the direction of Montluçon. The bus arrived ten minutes later. Tati got in. He handed her her baskets. The door banged.

Then, hands in pockets, he went back unhurriedly, remembering to stop and see whether there would be a big crop of nuts that year.

He did not know that this was the beginning of no ordinary day, or that he was living his last carefree moments. Not merely carefree! It was something more miraculous than that and the miracle had lasted a week and more. Hours, whole days, of innocence!

He was no longer any particular age! He was no longer this or that! He was not even a Passerat-Monnoyeur anymore!

He was Jean, like any child playing by the roadside, heedless of the future as of the past! Like a child, he cut a stick! Like a child gleefully anticipating a promised game, he kept saying to himself: "Let her be there."

In truth, ever since a heavy door, down there at Fontevrault, had shut behind him, ever since a man in uniform had called out: "Good luck" to him, ever since he had started walking straight ahead, aimlessly, he had had no more ties, everything had been a free gift, the days no longer counted, nothing counted except the magnificent present humming with sunshine.

He went through the kitchen to go and wash in the yard, which he did with care. The water was cool. He let it run over the back of his neck as he whetted his wiry hair; the soap stung his eyes and he sluiced himself down, soaping his chest, his back, his thighs.

From time to time he heard a touching trumpet call: on the toy canal a toy barge announcing that it was nearing the lock, and the wooden-legged man would stump along to open the gates.

He knew how to set about making his approach. He had a plan. And if the insurance man did come, it would be just too bad!

He crossed the bridge over the canal, then the one over the Cher. He penetrated into the brush of the sloping embankment and, clutching at the brambles, followed the bed of the river. When he caught sight of the pink daub of color made by the brickyard he forded the river on stepping-stones, his only fear being that he might make a sound.

After which he lay down in the long grass and began to crawl.

He was annoyed with himself for being late, for Félicie was already there. He could hear her voice. He was longing to see her and crawled more quickly, a blade of grass between his lips.

"The wolf . . . the wolf . . . the great big wolf! . . . Hooooo! . . ."

This was perhaps twenty yards from the low house, above which a trickle of smoke rose straight into the air, for there was not a breath of wind.

"Look out! . . . I'm the great big wolf. . . . Hoooooo!"

Still wearing her blue smock, with next to nothing beneath it except perhaps a slip, she crawled, then made a sudden jump.

"I'll eat you . . . I'll eat you . . . I'll eat you. . . ."

And the baby, sitting on the grass, gave a cry of mingled pleasure and fear, then burst into a laugh which went on so long it brought tears to his eyes. She rolled him over on the ground, nibbling at his knees, his calves, and his thighs, and his plump little bottom was naked to the sun.

"Again?"

She got up and Jean could see her standing there, her nostrils quivering, her eyes powdered with gold dust. She swept back her hair. In one deep breath she seemed to fill her lungs with all the joy of summer, and she took a few steps, crouched, put her hands on the ground.

"Look out! . . . The wolf . . . the wolf . . . the great big wolf! . . . Hoooooo! . . ."

The child, in rapt suspense, ceased to breathe. He was waiting for the moment when she would jump. He foresaw it almost to a second and gave his cry of pleasure and fear.

"I'll eat you . . . I'll eat you . . . I'll eat you. . . ."

Their laughter mingled together The child rolled in the grass. His little fingers clung to his mother's tawny hair, then, scarcely calmed down, he tried to utter syllables which meant, "Again . . ."

And Félicie began all over again. Time didn't count. There was the sound of the murmuring Cher and now and then the squeaking of a crank—the one that worked the lock gates—

and the stumping of the lock-keeper's wooden leg. Françoise, behind her house, a sack pinned in front of her by way of apron, her bare feet thrust into sabots, was plunging her arms into a tub of soapy water and washing clothes, throwing them out onto the grass where they made a great soft heap.

"The wolf . . . the great big wolf . . . the——"

She froze, her pupils suddenly fixed, suddenly cold. She had just spied Jean's face in the long grass behind her son.

He thought she was going to snatch up the baby and rush off to the house. And the thought that he frightened her was not all that disagreeable. Wasn't everyone in the district frightened of him, because he had been in Fontevrault and was forbidden by law to live outside a given distance?

They didn't know him. They had no means of learning. One day, when she was tamed, he would explain to her, very gently . . .

She was looking him in the eyes. Surely she was not afraid, since she did not think of protecting the baby lying between them?

All of a sudden, just when he least expected it, she stuck out her tongue at him.

He smiled. All he had to do was to get up, move toward her, speak to her. But she had got to her feet first, she had bent over the child and hoisted it onto her arm, and it was in that pose that she looked her youngest and most fragile.

He got up also. Before he was fully on his feet, she passed close by him, spat on the ground, and uttered, "Dirty dog!"

Then, without hurrying, without looking around, she made her way to where her mother was doing her washing.

As arranged, he waited for the bus at the side of the main road. He helped Tati get down and carried the greater bulk of the parcels. She had frowned on seeing him, and as soon as they were on the sunken path, she asked, "What's the matter with you?"

"Nothing."

"Did somebody come?"

"No."

How had she guessed that there was something wrong, when it was so intangible? What was there, in fact? Félicie was not frightened of him! It was not because he was fresh from prison that she made off as soon as she saw him!

She had spat on the ground. She had let fall, "Dirty dog!"

That was quite different. That was meant for the man who lived at Tati's, the man who was Tati's lover.

Tati, panting because he was walking too fast, still questioned with a searching, suspicious gaze: "Félicie didn't come?"

He could say no without lying. He was not curious to know what there was in the packages. His day had been spoiled, and perhaps far more than his day; his sky had been smirched; he did not feel like whistling any more; he was not hungry; he did not sniff, as on other days, at the already familiar smell of the kitchen.

"I've ordered a second incubator!" Tati announced as she took off her hat.

In her, too, there was something different, and he had the feeling that suddenly there was between them a certain distance which she hesitated to span.

"Aren't you going to ask me what I bought for you? Come, Jean! Let me see your face in the light. You remember what you told me the other day and what I answered?"

"What did I say?"

Instead of answering, she announced, "Just a while ago, a little before the end of market, a car stopped opposite the Hôtel de France. You do know the Hôtel de France, don't you?"

"Yes, I know it."

"It was a big open car, the sort there aren't many of in these parts. Inside there was a man and a woman. The woman was very pretty and very young and wearing an almost white suit. As the man got out, he murmured, 'I've only got five minutes, darling.'

"You know who it was?"

He frowned. He had a vague inkling, but he wasn't paying attention to the conversation.

"Let me look at you. His hair grew low on the forehead, like yours, but *his* hair was silvery. And his eyebrows met over the bridge of his nose, like yours. Why did you let it go when I said you weren't the son of Monsieur Passerat-Monnoyeur?"

"I said I was his son."

"And I told you it wasn't true."

"It doesn't matter."

She thought it better to open the parcels.

"Look! I've brought you back a razor, a shaving brush and some shaving soap. You take a sixteen collar, don't you? Here are three shirts. You'd better try one on, because I can take them back if they don't fit."

Some canvas shoes. Two packages of cigarettes. A belt with a metal buckle and a pair of blue denim trousers.

"Pleased?"

A kind of void was growing between them, now that she had mentioned the distiller.

"Where's Couderc?"

"He must be with the cows."

"Help me lay the table. I'll take my things off later."

And then, as she moved her saucepans about: "I know now who it is they call their lawyer. It's Bocquillon: a one-time law clerk who married a hunchback and set up a real-estate business. I've been to see him. I told him I'd pay him better than they would and he told me the whole story. If they can find a doctor to certify the old man is insane. . . ."

She looked at him in surprise. "What's the matter with you?

You're not the same as usual. I noticed it as I got off the bus. It's not because of your father?"

He did his best to laugh.

"Anyone would say you were depressed, or coming down with something. What did you do this morning?"

"Nothing."

"Did you stake the peas?"

"Yes."

"Did you feed the rabbits?"

"Yes."

"The insurance man didn't come?"

"No."

That was that! She put off till later the trouble of trying to understand. Old Couderc had come in noiselessly and sat down in his place. She unpacked some sausage, which she brought back from town every Saturday.

"The women all think the incubator won't work, or the chickens will die as soon as they're hatched. I got some hints from someone who rears chickens wholesale. All we've got to do is set up a brooder in the laundry. I've ordered one, the kind that burns charcoal...."

She could tell that he was not listening, that he was eating perfunctorily. She must go on waiting. After the meal the old man would go off. She would pour the coffee into her glass. She would let the sugar dissolve, push back her chair....

She had unhooked her black silk blouse, revealing a flannel slip and a bit of white flesh.

"Well, I've told you everything. I don't know yet how it will go with Bocquillon, but if things don't work out I'll get somebody else. I'll fight to the finish, even if it means setting fire to the house. What did you say?"

"I didn't say anything."

"If I get him to sign a paper now, Bocquillon says it would be worthless. A will can always be fought, especially when it's made by a man like Couderc. What do *you* think of him?"

"I don't know."

Her look reproached him for his inertia, for this absent-mindedness, as it were, which created a void in the kitchen.

"Well, I'll tell you my honest opinion. Couderc is not such a fool, or so far gone as he looks. I don't claim he can hear properly, but he guesses what people are saying from the way their lips move. He's a clever old devil. He doesn't want to make life difficult for himself. He has his vices. That's all he thinks of. He knows that so long as he keeps acting stupid no one can get at him. You saw him the other day with his two daughters. . . .

"If he lived with them, he'd be kept under watch. I bet it wouldn't be long before they put him in the asylum and the old monkey knows it, too. . . .

"Do you understand?

"With me, he can have his fun from time to time. He isn't ashamed.

"And those bitches would like to throw me out of the house! Let him have an accident tomorrow and they'll put the house up for sale. They have a right to, Bocquillon warned me. And I, the one who's done everything here, working like a horse all my life and putting up with the old man, I get exactly one third, one third of what, by rights, belongs to me, because if they had had the house, the sheriff would have been here long since to take the lot. . . ."

"What are you thinking about?"

"I'm not thinking."

It was true. He simply had an uneasy feeling, like somebody coming down with the flu. He was not digesting his lunch. He felt hot.

"It bothers me a little that you're the son of Monsieur

Passerat-Monnoyeur. To think that my sister was in service there! You must have known her."

"How long ago?"

"Ten years."

"Her name wasn't Adèle?"

"Yes. Why?"

"Nothing. I remember. She used to loathe my sister. Now I think my sister is married to a doctor at Orléans."

"He's a surgeon. Dr. Dorman."

Silence. The time had come when they ought to have been getting up from the table. There was no coffee left in the coffeepot, nor in the glasses.

"Will you get the brandy from the cupboard?...You don't mind me ordering you about and talking to you so familiarly....?"

"Why should I?"

"I don't know. Don't pour out so much for me...that's enough! You can help yourself to a big glass. How old are you?"

"Twenty-eight."

Her hands folded across her stomach, her eyes staring at the sparkling windowpanes and the dusty road beyond, she murmured:

"So that would make you twenty-three when....Just René's age now. When René did what he did, he was only nineteen. Tell me, Jean..."

"What?"

"Was it a man you killed?"

"A man, yes."

"Old?"

"I think he was in his fifties."

"Did you do it with a revolver?"

He shook his head and looked at his hands.

"Does it bother you that I talk about it?"

No! It didn't annoy him. He knew he would have to put up with it sometime or another. But it was all so far away! And so different from what people might imagine.

"You don't want to tell me? *I* tell you everything."

So he said, like someone reciting a lesson, "It began in the Boulevard St. Michel, in a beerhouse called the Mandarin. I don't know if it's still there."

"You were a student?"

Of course! And his father, since his wife's death . . . But what was the use of telling her all that?

"You had a mistress?"

Poor Tati, feeling jealous of Zézette! A mistress, yes, that being the customary name! She was kept by an engineer from the Creusot armament works. Was Tati any the wiser now?

"You were in love with her?"

He did not know now whether he had been in love with her, but he had certainly been jealous.

"'*Swear you'll never see your engineer again. . . .*'

"'*You're silly, Jean!*'"

It was her word. She was younger than he was, yet she felt she had to assume a protective tone, to kiss him on the eyes, and to say over and over again:

"'*You're silly!*'"

Or, at those moments when the heart opens:

"'*My darling idiot.*'"

She would give him almost motherly advice.

"'*It's crazy for you to get mixed up with a woman like me. . . . What difference can it make to you if Victor comes to see me now and then, if he pays the rent and my dressmaker's bills?*'"

That was enough to make him wild. He'd write to his father, to his sister. He'd invent every possible excuse to get them to send him money.

"'*You're spending too much. . . . Why did you order champagne again?*'"

Because people were looking at them, that was all! And she, why did she always contrive to get her bills presented in his presence?

All that was far away and confused. He could barely recall the gardens of the Luxembourg, the benches on which he used to wait for her for hours at a time, an unopened textbook on his knee. Then the evenings when neither of them knew what to do! The games of backgammon in a corner of the Mandarin, downstairs, where others were playing poker.

Tati realized that all this had gone on in a world unknown to her, but she made an effort to understand.

"So it was money you killed for, then?"

"I owed three months' rent, besides a squirrel coat I'd given her for a present and hadn't paid for. I was afraid she'd take her engineer back. I knew she was writing to him on the sly. I wonder now whether she wasn't seeing him now and again. She lied as she breathed. She'd say to me:

" *'You'd much better work for your exams. If I were your father . . .'*

"I begged my father to send me money. He spent hand over fist on his own mistresses. I was entitled to my mother's share of the estate, but he had sworn he would disown me if I claimed it.

"One evening, when I had just sold my watch, I saw some people, in the basement of the Mandarin, sitting down to a big game of poker.

"Actually, it wasn't my watch I'd sold, but a gold stopwatch I'd stolen from my father the last time I'd been to see him. I'd got three thousand francs for it. It was worth three times as much.

"Three thousand francs wasn't enough for me. . . .

"One of the poker players was a big man, fresh from his province, a contractor in Le Mans. He was losing. He was furious. My friends who were playing with him kept winking at me. . . ."

Tati gave a sigh like someone at a movie who feels the approach of the climax.

"I was with Zézette. She was wearing her squirrel coat. She said:

"'*I'll bet your friends are cheating. They're going to skin him, and it'll serve him right. The man's sure to have a wife and children....*'

"She had a strong respect for family....

"'*Don't play, Jean. What good will it do you? You're drinking too much and you'll be ill again. A fine thing for me, having to spend the night taking care of you, like last Tuesday.*'"

"You lost?" asked Tati, fiddling with her empty glass.

Unconsciously, her tone had become more formal.

"First he won my three thousand francs. I kept on ordering drinks. I insisted on playing on word of honor. I signed I.O.U.s. I lost ten thousand francs in less than an hour, and the man crowed with a fat laugh:

"'*I've got my shirt back! I've got my shirt back...and Papa Passerat-Monnoyeur will do the paying!...He can afford it. I've drunk enough of his liquor for that!*'

"When the game broke up, Zézette had left. Outside, it was drizzling. It might have been two o'clock in the morning, and the last cafés were closing.

"The man went out. I followed him at a distance. I had nothing special in mind. He crossed the Ile de la Cité and walked along the embankment. Then he crossed a bridge, at the tip of the Ile Saint-Louis, and I hurried up to him.

"'*Listen,*' I said, '*even if you won't give me back my three thousand francs, you've got to let me have at least the I.O.U.s I gave you.*'

"He began to laugh. I must have looked pale and tense, for his laughter grew less natural and I realized from his glance that he was afraid, that he was looking around for help....

"At that time, like a great many students, I used to carry brass knuckles in my pocket, for fun....

"The man was still laughing when I hit him, right in the face, and he went down in a heap."

"He was dead?" asked Tati, her bosom heaving.

Jean shrugged. "I took his wallet. I put it in my pocket. I got out fast.... Then..."

"He wasn't dead?..."

So he shouted, "No! Damn it, no! He was not dead! Or rather...how could I know?...I was already a hundred, two hundred yards away. Suddenly, I thought he'd be coming to, that a policeman on his beat would find him, and that he would report me. I retraced my steps. Only then did I feel any fear. I bent over him. He groaned...."

"As quickly as I could, I lifted him up, God knows how, he was so heavy, and hoisted him over the parapet...."

"There was fourteen thousand francs in the wallet and a snapshot of two children, twins, cheek to cheek...."

"Did they catch you right away?"

He lowered his head.

"Four months after. The body wasn't found until five weeks later, at a dam. The investigation took place without my name being mentioned."

"What about Zézette?"

"I'm sure she suspected the truth. I spent the fourteen thousand francs on her. One morning, the concierge came to me full of mystery to announce that the police had been to inquire about me....

"I disappeared. I slept at a friend's. The uncle he lived with could not be allowed to know I was in the house. I dared not go out anymore. During the day, I remained hidden under the bed. My friend would bring me leftovers, hard-boiled eggs, slices of cold meat....

"I wrote to my father asking for money to get abroad. He replied in one short phrase: 'Go to hell!'

"And so, one morning when I found I was beginning to

cough, I went to the quai des Orfèvres to give myself up. They didn't know who I was and left me in the waiting room for two hours.

"I was given a court-appointed counsel. He advised me to say that the man had tumbled over the parapet as I hit him, and that's what I said.

"Nobody believed it, but they gave me the benefit of the doubt and I only got five years...."

Tati's voice asked, "It didn't do anything to you?"

"What?"

"Killing him."

"I don't know anymore....I don't think so...." he said, looking out of the window.

The truth, the real truth, was that it wasn't his contractor he was thinking of as his brow clouded, but of his ruined day, of Félicie's spitting at him, of something that had existed and that he could not recapture.

"Don't drink any more...." murmured Tati, taking the bottle away from him.

He ran his hand over his face and sighed. "I'm sleepy."

"Go and lie down."

"Yes...I think...."

He climbed the stairs heavily, slumped down on his paillasse with its smell of musty hay. Cool air was coming in through the open skylight over his head, and with it the cackling of the chickens and the scraping of a rake someone was wielding somewhere—Couderc at the bottom of the garden, or the road mender on the towpath.

5

"*EVERY person condemned to death shall be decapitated.*"

He jumped up, as though, just when he thought himself alone, someone had laid a rough hand on his shoulder. The words had formed in his head, the syllables had written themselves in space, and he finished mechanically: "Article 12 of the Penal Code!"

It had been a mistake to sleep in the afternoon. Then, when he had gone downstairs again, Tati had looked at him overintently, as if there were some change in him. That look pursued him, in the darkness of the loft, under the moon-blue skylight.

"*Men condemned to forced labor shall be set to the hardest possible work; they shall wear an iron ball at their ankles and shall be joined in pairs by a chain. . . .*"

This time, it seemed to him that it was a cheerful voice that finished with: "Article 15 of the Penal Code."

The voice of his counsel, Maître Fagonet, who was twenty-eight and looked younger than Jean. He used to come into the cell, air puffing the folds of his black gown, a faint aroma of apéritif on his lips, on which still lingered traces of the smile he had given to his girlfriend as he left her in the car a hundred yards from the prison.

"Well, old boy? What story are we going to tell dear Oscar today?"

The name of the examining magistrate was Oscar Darrieulat. Maître Fagonet found it more fun to call him Oscar.

"Have you brushed up on your Article 305?"

The recollection was so clear, the presence of Fagonet so real, that Jean had to sit up in his bed, his eyes wide open to the darkness, his chest heaving as it had when, as a child, he would throw himself out of the bedclothes, in the grip of a nightmare.

The extraordinary thing was that it was years since any of this had come back to him. More so: at the time when these events were unfolding in reality, he had taken scarcely any heed of them.

It had been too complicated. They harried him with questions. His counsel kept repeating articles of the Code incessantly.

"'*Murder shall entail the death penalty when it precedes, accompanies or follows another crime....*' Do you understand, young man, why you must not at any price admit the story of the wallet?"

It was not tragic, not at the time. Even his warder would toss him each morning a cheerful, "Slept well?"

And the examining magistrate, the famous Oscar, was courteous, with an air of not wishing to press certain details.

"Sit down.... So you say that he struck you first, not hard enough, however, to leave any mark. For my own part, I'm willing to accept this. Only, it's the others who've got to be convinced, isn't it?"

His wife would telephone him during the interview. He would answer:

"Yes, darling. Yes, darling. All right. I won't forget. Yes, seven pounds..."

Seven pounds of what?

"*Every person condemned to death shall be decapitated.*"

He turned heavily on his bed, his nerves taut.

"Article 321, old man. But for Article 321 we'd be done. That's what I'm going to plead.... But if you can't help me...."

"*Murder, as also wounds and blows, is justifiable if provoked by blows or violent assault against the person.*"

Maître Fagonet ran a little comb through his thick and glossy hair.

"You have joined him on the bridge without any evil intentions. All you want to do is ask him to give you back part of the money he's won off you. You tell him about Zézette. He laughs in your face. You make a move and he thinks you mean to strike him. He strikes first. You lose your head, and in the struggle you push him over the parapet."

In a different tone of voice, Maître Fagonet pronounced, "They won't believe us."

"What then?"

"We shall get the benefit of the doubt."

Sometimes he would tell the prisoner the story of the play he had seen the night before at the theater.

The trial itself had unfolded like a play. People looked at him curiously. He'd catch himself looking at them while his thoughts were elsewhere.

"Gentlemen, the Court!"

And now, suddenly, years later, lying on his paillasse with its smell of musty hay, here he was realizing at last that it was serious, that it was grave, that his head had really been at stake.

"*Every person condemned to death shall...*"

He would have liked to get up, to go downstairs near Tati, not to be alone. He was afraid. He was drenched with sweat and he had the impression that something, his heart no doubt, was not functioning properly in his chest.

"You see before you, gentlemen of the jury, a youth, the victim of..."

Of what? Of none of the things Maître Fagonet had said! And already, while the lawyer spoke and flapped his black wings, Jean wanted to shake his head.

"One...two...three...four...five..."

The drops of water dripped from the white cheese. He would have liked to cry out, because his brain kept on working, because images kept going through his head, too sharp, super-imposed one upon another, accompanied by voices and sensations like that of the sunbeam which, in the courtroom, reached his left hand, just his left hand and no more, in a little quivering disk.

None of it was true, any more than the story he had told Tati. The truth—the truth which he alone knew—was that it had all begun when he was fourteen and that the real culprit, really, was his English teacher.

Jean had forgotten his name. It was odd, forgetting that, when the other details were so vivid. A man carved in wood, with a pale face, big dark eyes, and a black mustache, who wore a jacket that was too long for him and looked more like a frock coat.

"Monsieur Passerat-Monnoyeur..."

Pronouncing Jean's name, he assumed a different voice and the pupils would all feel a cold chill down the spine. The window was open onto the school garden. A woman was beating her carpets at a second-floor window.

"I imagine that it would be pointless for me to ask you a question, eh?...The son of Monsieur Passerat-Monnoyeur is wealthy enough to have no need to earn his living and he is not required to be intelligent...."

Sharp little teeth appeared for a moment beneath the mustache. The master was satisfied. He collected a few smiles from the class.

"You may sit down, Monsieur Passerat-Monnoyeur. I regret that the rules do not allow me to send you out for a walk during my period. Nevertheless, I regard you as not being present."

And, when he collected their compositions, he'd keep Jean's separate, walk slowly up to the fire and throw it in with affectation, making as if to warm his hands.

Whose fault was it? His father's: he was too elegant and the English master kept seeing him drive around in his car and seldom without some pretty girl next to him.

He took no interest in his son. If Jean happened to get up late, he had only to go to the office.

Dear Sir,

May I ask you kindly to excuse my son who was unable to go to school yesterday on account of a slight indisposition which necessitated his remaining in bed.

That year, Jean had made himself ill so as not to have to take his examinations. He had spent the whole month of July in the garden of the house, up on the hill, and in the end he was dragging himself around like a really sick person and moving with the caution of an invalid.

The following year he had been kept back in the fourth form. He did no work. He knew that from now on it was useless. He had given up.

He was taller and thinner than his schoolmates, more elegant, and since he always had pocketfuls of money, he used to stand them ice cream.

When his wallet happened to be empty, he would take a few odd notes from the petty cash, and there was no one but the old bookkeeper to notice it.

He had given up trying to do anything. Twice he had failed to get his degree, and he had only gotten it in the end by influence.

That was how it had come about. He loved to stroll idly about the streets with friends, to eat ice cream, and, later on, to drink beer at sidewalk cafés.

Sometimes anguish would seize him by the throat: what would become of him if?...

Nothing! Nothing would become of him. He had given up. It was too late!

He got up and remained standing barefoot in the middle of the loft, trying to cool off.

"*Every person condemned to death shall...*"

It was throbbing, painful, unexpected. Living through the tragedy, the trial, and prison, he had scarcely realized that it was himself it was happening to. He listened to the presiding judge putting questions to the witnesses.

"Raise your right hand. Swear to tell the truth, the whole truth, and nothing but the truth. You are neither a relative of the prisoner nor..."

The feeling that all this array was so utterly out of scale with himself! How could so much fuss be made over nothing at all?

They argued over his case as if he had been a man, a man responsible for his actions, and on his bench, between his two gendarmes, he felt himself to be still at school!

His father had not come. Nor his sister. True, at that time she was not yet twenty.

"Raise your right hand. Swear...."

At the adjournment, they went out to smoke cigarettes in the corridors or drink a glass of beer in the bar! In the evening, they went home!

"*Every person condemned to death shall...*"

He bit his lip. He was aching all over. The agony took him at some undefined point and spread to his whole being, right down to the ends of his fingers, of his toes, which went rigid as if seized by cramp.

Why had Tati looked at him like that? At times it was as though she understood, at others as though she were still trying to understand.

No one had pitied the fate of the contractor from Le Mans, although he had two children. Jean had felt no pity either. He had never had any remorse. He scarcely remembered him: rather he remembered a mass, bulky because of a heavy woolen overcoat.

"It must not be forgotten, gentlemen of the jury, that when my client made his unfortunate gesture, he was in an advanced state of intoxication, and..."

That was not true either. He had been drinking, but he was clearheaded. He was even more clearheaded than usual.

Better still! Coming out of the Mandarin behind the contractor, he had made a distinct pause, and had said to himself, "You're going to do something stupid."

He could have gone away. And, if he had not done so, was it not precisely because he wanted to be done with it all? Was it not because he was sick at heart, because he had had enough?

He wanted something definite and final, something that offered no prospect of retreat.

Indeed, in the very instant of striking out with the brass knuckles, it was the face of his English master he thought he saw before him.

He had made off, very calm, almost relieved. He was on the far side of the bridge when he turned and saw the dark mass lying on the stones.

Once again, he had hesitated. Would it not be simpler to throw the man into the water? That would avoid complications in the morning. He'd be left alone.

He had walked back almost nonchalantly. He had bent down. Why not?

"Every person condemned to death shall..."

And it was now, so many years afterwards, now when nothing was at stake anymore, that he knew fright, a retrospective, poignant consuming fright. He walked as far as the door. He wanted to go downstairs, to go into Tati's room, to sit down on the foot of her bed. She would understand that he needed company.

What had become of Maître Fagonet? He had always appeared cordial toward Jean, who had, unwittingly, brought him his first case. At the end, they were on the best of terms and the lawyer would tell him tales about his love affairs.

He lifted the glass of the skylight. Air came through. He heard the calls of birds, night birds no doubt. He knew nothing about birds.

He felt suddenly cold, and threw himself down on his bed.

Why had he been so happy only the night before, and why, all of a sudden...?

He had a headache, and, having dropped off to sleep only toward morning, he found it difficult to wake. Tati realized it at first glance. "Not feeling so good? Go and drink a cup of coffee before you feed the hens."

She was perhaps the first creature on earth to understand him. From that first Saturday on the bus, when she had no idea who he was or what he had done, she had spoken to him familiarly. In reality, she had never taken him for a grown-up.

"Do this! Do that! Go and wash! Go and shave! Drink a cup of coffee."

And she watched him come and go, keeping her thoughts to herself. If he should fall sick, she might very well lift him in her arms like a child, put him to bed, turn him this way and that, undress him, poultice him.

"Lie still. This must be done."

Indeed that was exactly what he had always wanted—to be ill in that fashion. At home they would have sent one of the maids to him, or the doctor, or even a full-fledged nurse.

"It's my fault, eh?" she said suddenly as he stooped over the incubator to trim the lamp.

"What is?"

"I shouldn't have talked to you about it."

He bluffed: "It's all one to me...."

He measured out the bran and the grits, poured in the warm water, mixed the mash.

Tati contrived not to leave him alone that morning.

"Saturday, you will come to market with me. It'll make a change for you. Besides, it's time you went to the barber's. Your hair is already so long it makes a roll at the back of your neck."

He would have liked to cross the canal, to lie down in the long grass and watch Félicie. He had to be content with the distant view of the pink roof and its trickle of smoke.

Once, when he was only twelve, he had had a spot on the lung. The doctor was worried and had him X-rayed to make sure there were no tubercular lesions. A schoolmate of his was in a sanatorium at Leysin.

And he had longed, so ardently, to be attacked by lesions. He too would go up there in the mountains. He would have nothing to do. He would lie in a deck chair—that was his picture of sanatorium life—facing the mountains, and everything would be taken care of for him, food would be dropped into his mouth as though he were a puppy or a nestling, everyone would be kind, attentive to his slightest need, while he would be able to dream from morning till night.

"Nothing whatever, young fellow. Your lungs are absolutely sound."

Tati looked at the time regretfully. "I must go to church."

It was Sunday once again. He had not noticed the anglers along the canal, or the increased number of bicycles.

"*Every person condemned to death...*"

He ought to have been condemned to death. He knew that. Article 314.

"*Murder shall entail the death penalty when it precedes, accompanies or follows another crime.*"

That was his case. The theft of the wallet. In any case, Article 304 provided precisely for the situation:

"*Murder shall equally entail the death penalty when it has for its object either the preparation, facilitation or execution of an offense, or assisting the flight or insuring the impunity of those who have committed the said offense or of their accomplices.*"

In other words, if he had not lied, if he had not sworn that the contractor had struck the first blow and in the struggle fallen into the river...

"Tati!" he called.

He had gone up as far as the door of her bedroom, while she dressed for church.

"What's the matter?"

"Nothing."

He had nearly confessed: "I'm afraid."

Never had he felt such a longing to be ill. Why not go to church with her? That would perhaps give him a chance to think of something else?

"You'll keep an eye on the fire, won't you? Don't put the potatoes on till half-past eleven. Here, hook up my dress! Try not to pinch the skin."

He was left all alone. He did not know where the old man was. He pushed open the dining-room door, but not to steal the money in the tureen. It was for the sole pleasure of opening up this room where never foot was set. The door, as it opened, made a noise somewhat like a cork coming out of a bottle. The air, which was never disturbed, was suddenly displaced, thicker than elsewhere, and it could be felt moving across one's cheek. The very things in the room, like the tureen, set fast in the silence and their own immobility, seemed to quiver.

Whose wedding present, long ago, had been the paper-thin white metal bowl standing in the middle of the table runner?

He had paid no attention to the throbbing of an engine. He had heard it, but he hadn't thought that it could have anything whatever to do with him. Now he gave a start on hearing footsteps on the tiled floor of the kitchen, and a woman's voice calling, "Anybody in?"

The blind was always down in the dining room–museum. That was why Jean had to blink when he left the half darkness to go into the kitchen, where the door was open to the sunlight.

He was wearing his blue denim trousers, a white shirt open across his chest, and canvas shoes. As Tati had observed, his hair made a thick roll on the nape of his neck.

He saw a young woman standing there, wearing a light dress and a colored hat, and carrying a small handbag. He was about to ask a question, any question, when he recognized her, at the very moment when she lifted her handkerchief to her eyes.

"Billie!"

She was shaking her head, to convey that she could not speak. She was sniffling. He brought a straw-bottomed chair for her, and she sat down on it mechanically, with that reserved dignity people assume in deep grief.

He was not moved. He noticed things he would never have expected to notice on seeing his sister again after so many years: for instance, he admired her shoes, very beautiful custom-made shoes she must have ordered from a leading shoemaker. Her stockings were sheer, the seams neat and straight. His sister Billie had always been well dressed and well groomed.

Still sniffling a little, she shook her head once more, ventured a quick look.

"I can't explain how it makes me feel..."

She was telling herself that perhaps it would be proper to kiss him, but at the same time she was thinking that he was a murderer. And that changed everything. He was no longer, in fact, an ordinary man. He impressed her. He had grown in stature.

"Even though I was prepared...I had had a letter....But seeing you here, all of a sudden, in this kitchen..."

"The last time we met..."

Evidently she remembered, for she blushed.

"It was in your bedroom."

A lovely room, a real rich girl's room, blue and white, complete with fur rugs.

"You didn't want to be seen because you had a pimple on your nose. I had come to ask you for a little money."

She had been only seventeen then, and her father gave her as much money as she wanted. It was less trouble than giving other things. The loveliest dresses. The loveliest hats. Holidays at the loveliest seaside resorts, in the best hotels. Their house was the loveliest in Montluçon.

"Why do you remind me of that, Jean? I was so far from suspecting——"

"That I really needed it. You've changed, you know. You used to be plump, with a big bosom that was your despair. Now, you're slender."

"I have two children."

"Ah!"

She was going to put her bag on the table, hesitated.

"It's quite clean," he said. "Wait a second..."

He got a cloth out of the cupboard and wiped the scrubbed wooden table top.

"Won't you have something to drink? A cup of coffee? A glass of brandy?"

"Jean!"

"What?"

"I don't know.... I don't know how to speak to you."

She was eyeing the coarse cloth of his trousers, the canvas shoes, the long hair through which he would run his fingers when a lock fell down over his forehead. He looked so utterly at ease, so utterly at home in this kitchen!

"You're married, aren't you?"

She smiled nervously.

"Since I have two children...."

"That doesn't signify! Your husband is not with you?"

He went and leaned out of the door and saw a handsome car parked a hundred yards from the house, in the shade of the hazels.

"He's taken the opportunity to call on one of his colleagues at St. Amand."

She fiddled nervously with her handkerchief.

"I'm to pick up Philippe on my way back."

"Of course!"

"Why do you say *of course*?"

"Nothing . . . You still see Father?"

"Have people been telling you things?"

"What would they have told me? You were his pet. You could twist him around your little finger. . . . Has he married again?"

Now! This was more like his sister. She was looking at him with suspicious eyes, quite sure that the words hid something, and it made him smile. He preferred this to her tears.

"Listen, Jean. . . ."

"What must I listen to?"

"Don't answer like that. It's so obviously not natural. It's like a grating cog."

"I swear, Billie, I'm not grating. You've come. That means you have something to tell me. Is it so difficult?"

She dabbed at her eyes to avoid having to answer at once. Then, looking at the doors: "There's nobody here?"

"Tati's at church. I don't know where the old goat is."

"The old goat?"

"That's what we call him. Forget it. So, you were saying that father? . . ."

And he went to the mantelpiece and took the old pipe of Couderc's he had cleaned with brandy the Sunday before.

6

"IF YOU think I've come as an enemy, I'd better go. It's not my fault if seeing you here. . . ."

"Isn't it all right here?"

She, of course, would be living in a house in the same style as their father's. A new, modern villa, on a hillside. The builder had had it photographed from all angles, so that he could show it off, in color, in his catalogues, so closely did it correspond to people's notion of happiness.

Everything was bright. The light came in through wide bays and the windows opened by means of well-oiled cranks in a white metal as fine as silver. Clumps of flowers flanked the terrace, where coffee and liqueurs were always served.

People passing by on the road would glance over the gate. They glimpsed the three-car garage, the chauffeur forever busy polishing his cars, the lawns, a revolving sprinkler, the gardener stooping over his flower beds.

And beyond, under the huge red overhanging roof, on the shady terrace, brightly clad people sitting around and sipping pleasant drinks.

A squeaking sound, outside. Billie cocked an ear, but Jean reassured her.

"It's nothing. Just someone working the drawbridge. Must be a motorboat, because the barges don't move on Sundays."

"Answer me frankly, Jean. Is it because of Father you've come back in these parts? Have you seen him?"

"No."

She still did not believe him. She was distrustful.

"And you don't know he's married a girl two years younger than I am? A little thing who served behind the counter in a cake shop."

"It was bound to happen some time or another."

"What do you plan to do?"

"And you?"

"What do you mean, 'And you'? Honestly, Jean, I don't understand you. You're speaking words that have no meaning. You're paying no attention to the conversation. Are you waiting for someone?"

"No. I'm waiting for it to be half-past eleven so that I can put the potatoes on to boil."

"Did you suffer all that much?"

"When? When I found Father with Lucette?"

"What are you talking about?"

"Nothing. Just a picture that comes back to me, that has often come back to me. I think it settled a lot of things. Mother had just fallen ill...."

"You were barely nine years old!"

"Exactly. There was a bathroom next to her bedroom, then a huge closet where all the family's clothes were hung. The doctor hadn't been gone five minutes...he had hurt Mother and she was dozing off. I wanted to go into the closet and I caught Father there with Lucette. D'you want me to tell you what posture they were in?"

"Stop it!"

"Then, tell me why you've come."

"Well, we don't see Father anymore! There was a scene, a few days after his marriage. When I heard you were here, I thought you would be going to Montluçon."

"Why?"

"Don't play the fool, Jean! Father too must be expecting a visit from you. You won't get me to believe...."

As he put the potatoes on to boil, after fueling the stove, she got up abruptly, in the grip of extreme nervous tension.

"For heaven's sake, sit still! Stop acting this farce."

"What farce?"

"You want me to believe you really mean to stay on in this house? In what capacity are you here anyway?"

"Farmhand!"

"Farmhand! That's it."

"Do you want to see my chickens? In a few days, sixty chicks will hatch out in the incubator. . . ."

"And you don't intend to see our father, of course. You won't go and claim your share of Mother's legacy from him, will you?"

"I hadn't thought of it."

"Don't be clever with me, Jean. You know it won't go with me. I know you!"

"You think so?"

She stamped her foot impatiently.

"What are you doing in that cupboard?"

"I'm getting out the brandy and some glasses. I'm thirsty. Or would you prefer some black-currant juice?"

"I'm speaking seriously. If you insist on going your own way, that's your affair. But just you wait till you've seen Father—you'll tell a different story then."

"Have you been to see him?"

"I wrote to him."

"To claim your share of Mother's legacy?"

"We're in our rights. Philippe had to incur heavy expenses for his surgery. D'you know how Father reacted?"

"No!"

"He answered me by telephone. I knew he would take notice in the end. He swore that, so long as he lived, he wouldn't give us a penny. He claims that when he married Mother she had no money, and that everything he possesses he earned."

"Quite true."

"How dare you say such a thing?"

"After all, Mother was always ill. She couldn't have."

"That's no reason for denying us our legacy. Then, I thought that, since you would be going to see him..."

"No."

"What d'you mean, no?"

"I'm saying that I won't go."

"Perhaps you mean to spend the rest of your life in this house?"

"Perhaps I do."

"I think I had better go."

She wanted to cry. Nerves, as always. The least annoyance threw her in this state.

"I shall tell Philippe...."

"What will you tell him?"

"You hate us, don't you?"

Why did Article 12 come back to him like the refrain of a song?

"*Every person condemned to death shall be decapitated.*"

"I'm beginning to realize that you've come back to these parts only to aggravate us. You're not even discreet. You tell everybody your name. People were beginning to forget. They'll start talking again. Admit it—that's how you plan to set about making Father give you your money! It's deliberate, your dressing like a tramp and living with God knows what sort of people."

"With Tati."

"What did you say?"

"I'm saying I live with Tati. She's my mistress. Besides me there's the old goat, as she calls him. He's her father-in-law. From time to time she takes him to bed with her, like giving sweets to a child to keep it quiet. It's the only way of retaining the house...."

"Jean!"

"What?"

"This is painful. Do you really not understand? You're doing it on purpose, I know. But I came to help you. Philippe would have found you a job."

"Not too near here!"

"I beg you! Stop this constant joking. Do you want me to go down on my knees? I can feel that you're going to do some crazy thing again. You've started off on the wrong foot...."

"I always did start off on the wrong foot...."

"Be quiet. Listen to me. Just think that if Mother were here, she'd tell you the same."

"She'd ask me whether I was not too unhappy."

"And I? Isn't that just what I've been asking you for the past hour? Haven't I come to try and get you out of here? You're young. You have———"

"I have years of lost time to make up. At this moment, I ought to be dead, my head severed from my body...."

"Have you no pity, then, no feeling?"

"I'm tired."

He looked around for something to do and, picking up a piece of wood, he began to whittle it, with the slow and careful movements of a peasant.

"Shall I go?" asked his sister, not knowing what to do with herself any more.

He looked at her as if he did not see her and passed his hand across his brow.

"What a bore you are...." he sighed.

At the same moment he cocked an ear, took a few steps toward the door, with his bit of wood and his knife still in his hand.

"What is it?" he asked.

Félicie was rushing up, in her blue smock, her hair disheveled, terror in her eyes.

"Come quickly. Auntie ... Auntie ..."

He turned toward Billie, standing there in the half light of the kitchen. He wanted to say good-bye, but did not take the time.

"Well! . . . What's happened?"

"She's . . . she's hurt. . . . Come on. . . ."

At one stroke the sun had taken possession of him. Another world was swallowing them up—himself and Félicie running on ahead and too much shaken to be able to cry.

The anglers, along the canal bank, knew nothing. Bubbles broke the surface of the water. The pink roof, yonder . . . a dark doorway in a white wall . . .

"She doesn't stop bleeding. . . . I'm scared. . . . It was my father. . . ."

The wooden-legged lock-keeper was smoking his pipe, sitting on his doorstep while one of his brood crawled on all fours in front of him.

It might have been foreseen that things would take a turn for the worse one day, but not like this, not on a Sunday morning, in bright sunshine.

Tati, in her best black dress, had been on her way back along the canal, a little out of breath as she always was when walking. In one hand she was carrying her prayer book, in the other her umbrella. She used it as a sunshade on the sunlit parts of the path, but here the shade was almost cool under the chestnut trees lining both banks of the canal. Sometimes a bicycle passed her. Boys and girls pedaled along, laughing. Tati was talking to herself. That was a habit of hers.

And then, on reaching the lock, she stopped, her eyes suddenly hard. A hundred yards off she saw the drawbridge and, on it, two cows, her own, blocking the footway, and a little boy trying to drive them back.

To others this meant nothing, no more than a speck on the landscape. But Tati knew better and, instead of continuing on her way, she crossed the lock and marched straight on toward the little house in the brickyard.

Félicie, having bicycled back from church, had already changed and was playing with her baby near the doorstep. She straightened up to see her aunt go by.

Tati, without hesitation, without a moment's pause, walked straight into the kitchen and there in front of her, just as she had expected, she found old Couderc sitting at the table with a pot of wine. He had his hat on. The table was covered with a small-checked oilcloth.

Settled close to the fire, her legs slightly apart, Françoise was peeling potatoes, which she dropped one by one into a bucket.

It was calm as a lake, calm as a pond. But Tati broke this calm, crossed the kitchen, gripped the old man by the shoulder, pulling up the sleeve of his jacket. She knew he could not hear, but that did not stop her talking.

"Get out of here, you!...I suspected as much. As soon as my back's turned, people take advantage and start their little schemes...."

Then Françoise, who had always been placidity and stupidity personified, dropped the potato peelings out of her apron, stood up, and planted herself in the middle of the room. Black wool stockings showed under her too short skirt.

"You're the one who'll get out of here, my girl!" she announced with an anxious glance through the window curtains.

And, turning toward the door: "Félicie!... Call your father."

He was behind the house, digging a patch of earth which all winter long was strewn with yellowed leeks. He could be heard approaching in his sabots. He stamped them outside the door.

"What's this?" asked Tati. "What does this mean?"

"It means, my girl, that Father will stay here if he pleases and that you'll be the one to get out. Understand? Let her by, Eugène."

"So! You'd like to keep the old man. So that's what comes of all your scheming and whisperings with Amélie. Perhaps it was the lawyer who put you up to this? We'll soon see whether Couderc——"

And she grabbed the old man's arm, pulling at it. Françoise intervened. "I'm telling you he'll stay here with us."

"And I'm telling you, you bitch.... Let go of me, d'you hear?"

"I'll let go of you when you're out, you old bag."

"So! You——"

Unexpectedly, Tati snatched at her sister-in-law's bun and the hair came down.

"So! You want to keep the old man. So! You——"

"Mamma!" cried Félicie, who had come to peep through the door. "Mamma!"

"So! You——"

And Tati was pulling with all her strength. Françoise banged her knee against a chair and let out a cry.

"Eugène! Well! What are you——"

Félicie was crying. The old man was hugging the wall. Eugène, frowning, still hesitated to act.

When he did decide, it was to snatch up the bottle standing on the table.

"Let go of my wife!" he shouted. "Let go of my wife or else I'll——"

Then, suddenly, the bottle cracked on Tati's head and everyone froze into stillness, all movement suspended for a long moment.

Then Eugène looked down at the bottleneck still in his hand and appeared dumbfounded.

Tati herself had remained apparently stupefied for an instant. When she passed her hand across the top of her head, it came away red with blood and she felt her legs give under her.

She felt no pain, but the blood was flowing. It ran down her forehead, reached her eyelids, her nose, zigzagged round the corners of her lips before reaching her chin.

"Sit down," Françoise managed to utter. "Wait! Félicie!...
Félicie!...Run and get someone...do something....Now
you, you can be proud. Well! Are you going to stay stuck there
like the idiot that you are?...Perhaps we ought to cut off her
hair?...Tati!...Tati!..."

Tati had fainted. She was swaying. They caught her just as
she was about to fall to the ground and they laid her out on the
stone floor.

"Félicie!...Where are you?"

Félicie, leaving her baby forgotten on the grass, was running
along the canal.

"Hand me the vinegar, you fool!...No, not that! That's the
oil. Let's hope....You're not going to pass out, are you?"

Indeed, Eugène felt himself growing weak. He had to sit
down on a chair, and there he remained, plunged in his
thoughts, not daring to look at his sister-in-law.

When Jean entered, the kitchen smelled of vinegar; there
was a pool of blood on the floor and blood was spurting
through Tati's graying hair. She half opened her eyes, gave a
long sigh, called, as though she knew he was there, "Jean!...
Don't let them cut off my hair."

She was barely recognizable. She seemed fatter, and for a
moment he thought her head had swelled. It was the red of the
blood which distorted it so.

"Water," he ordered.

He was obeyed. Félicie brought towels from the next room.

If the gendarmes had appeared at that moment, Eugène
would have been quite ready to breathe, "I give myself up."

Françoise was just beginning to cry. Félicie wanted to be
sick. The lock-keeper, intrigued, observed the house from a distance, hesitating to walk so far on his wooden leg.

"I can't see where it is," murmured Jean.

And Tati: "Careful! You're hurting me. Don't you realize
you're tearing my skin!"

Her hair was matted. He was trying to catch sight of the wound, but could not manage to.

"We must cut it off," repeated Françoise, not knowing perhaps what she was saying.

Tati could not be so bad as all that, for she answered in her most cantankerous voice, "I'll cut *yours* off for you! Just you wait...."

And Jean announced: "It's nothing. A gash an inch long. It's bleeding a lot, but I don't think it's deep."

"Help me get up, Jean!"

"There's no hurry," Françoise intervened. "Take your time till you feel better. We'll give you a little drop.... Go and fetch something, Félicie."

"You won't catch me drinking anything in your house again!"

Things had already ceased to be tragic. Eugène was gaining his courage and, as his daughter had set a bottle on the table, he helped himself to a big glass.

Tati insisted on getting up. "Steady me, Jean...."

And Françoise: "It's really your fault! If you hadn't pulled me by the hair, like a ... like a ..."

She hesitated to use strong language to a woman who had just fainted.

"Like a what?"

"Nothing. It's all right.... Eugène didn't do it on purpose. As for Father, he has the right to——"

"Hold me, Jean. I think I'm going to fall. There's a pounding in my head."

"Come along."

Without Couderc? She still hesitated, turning toward him. However, she felt really ill. She was afraid of fainting again.

"I'm going now, but let them just wait...."

Outside, he saw tears start from her eyes, tears of vexation and rage.

"Is there still blood on my face?"

"Hardly any."

"People will wonder."

She walked faster, turning her head away when she passed near one of the anglers.

The two cows had finally crossed the bridge and were standing stupidly in front of the house, as if hesitant to enter the kitchen, the door of which was open.

At the far end of the path Jean saw his sister's car still parked. Billie was at the wheel. Evidently she wanted to find out what had happened.

They had scarcely got into the kitchen when she started the engine, let in the clutch, and maneuvered noisily back and forth several times in order to turn around in the narrow track.

"Has somebody been here?" asked Tati mechanically.

Billie's perfume still hung about the room.

"Help me to get to bed. There's a great pounding in my head. You really think there's nothing broken?"

"We can call the doctor."

"And what would the doctor do? Give me a shove. I feel like I'll never get to the top of the stairs. I'd never have thought a fool like Eugène could have. . . ."

There was a stale smell in the bedroom.

"Unhook my dress. Hurry up!"

He undressed her as one skins a rabbit. The black silk clung to her plump flesh. She had begun to cry softly.

"You're kind, Jean. Wait! I can get to bed on my own. Who was it that came?"

"My sister."

"What did she want?"

And then, suddenly sitting up on the bed: "You're not going to leave, are you? She didn't come to get you?"

"Lie still. Wait, now. . . . Are there any disinfectants in the house?"

"There must be some iodine in the cupboard...."

It was the first time he had looked after anyone. He was astonished to feel so nimble, with an eye for everything, and gestures quick and sure.

"Where are you going?"

"For some boiled water."

"Promise you're not going to leave."

"Of course I'm not."

"Promise!"

"I promise.... Hold this towel over your head so as not to mess the pillow...."

He could have wished his sister back again, so that she could see him moving about as though he were at home, poking up the fire, drawing water at the well, boiling it, opening a cupboard full of old dresses which smelled of mothballs, and searching for a little brown bottle.

From her bed, Tati listened for every noise, and the only thing she feared was a sudden silence.

"Get in, cows! Not that way, you dummies. We'll take care of you soon."

Would he be able to milk them? He had watched the old man do it, but had never tried.

When he returned to the bedroom, Tati enveloped him with a grateful, admiring look.

"What is it?" he asked.

"Nothing. You're funny like this. Anyone would say you'd been nursing all your life."

He had taken down a blue apron from behind the kitchen door.

"Now, try to keep still. I think I'm going to hurt you a bit, but it's got to be done."

"There's not much of it left, is there?"

"Of what?"

"My hair. It doesn't make you squeamish? Your shirt's covered with blood."

"If you don't keep still, I——"

"All right! But you're pulling at the skin."

He made her a bandage shaped like a turban which transformed her.

"I feel as weak as if—— What are you going to eat, Jean?"

"The potatoes are cooking."

"Just get yourself a slice of ham. A little later, I'll be able to get up. Pull the blind down, will you? The light hurts my eyes."

She snatched a furtive kiss on the back of his hand. He went downstairs, took a plate from the cupboard.

And, after he had eaten, he went and stood in the doorway, a cigarette between his lips, his hands in his pockets.

The Sunday strollers were beginning to invade the towpath where the shade from the trees looked purple.

"Perhaps I ought to take her up a cup of coffee?" he thought.

He had forgotten his terrors of the night. He was happy.

7

A WARM, soft rain fell from early morning till nightfall, and such calm, such silence, prevailed beneath the padded quilt of the sky that you felt you could hear the grass growing.

Noises, whether close or far off, did not, as in the sunshine, blend into a symphony, they soared, one by one, set in silence, with the quality of a solo or a personal message—be it the crowing of a cock, the clang of the crank handle dropped by the lock keeper after he had used it, or the thin blast of a barge's trumpet.

Jean had woken earlier than usual and he might, upon discovering the gloom through his skylight, have mistaken it for a shred of night. A cow lowing in the shed reminded him that Couderc was no longer there and that it was he who would, once again, torture the poor beasts.

But suddenly the silence was rent by a shrill, unexpected cry, coming from inside the house.

"Jean!"

The cry was agonized, dramatic. It called to mind one of those streetcar accidents by which a street, all light and gaiety a second before, is transformed into a hospital waiting room, or one of those haggard creatures rushing madly out of a house yelling, their eyes wide, "Fire!...There!...There!..."

Jean was almost frightened. Frightened of nothing specific. Frightened of tragedy. He started downstairs. Tati's door opened abruptly.

"Jean! Look!"

He could not see at once, because the light came from behind her.

"I'm going to die, Jean."

He had an unpleasant shock when he finally made out Tati's face, disfigured, her eyes nearly closed by swellings, her lips awry. Her head seemed to be twice its normal size, and, as she looked at herself in the glass, she stammered, "I'm getting water on the brain. I knew someone like that, with blood turning to water, but in the legs. What do you think, Jean? Am I going to die?"

And the curious thing about it was this: no sooner had he left the bedroom than he felt neither sad nor anguished. He had remembered to open the henhouse door as he went by. He had thrown a handful of grain to the poultry and felt a twinge of regret, as he crossed the kitchen, that there was no cold coffee left over from the night before.

Bareheaded, he walked along the canal, whose waters were as thick and smooth as black velvet. The people in the little house in the brickyard were up. Doubtless they were at the table, drinking their breakfast coffee? Only Françoise came and stood framed in the doorway, unkempt and unwashed, to watch him go by.

He grunted a good morning as he passed close to the wooden-legged lock-keeper, but he got no reply.

He stepped along as lightly as if he were out for a stroll. He overtook two children on their way to school. As he entered the grocery, which also sold tobacco and had a telephone booth, the doorbell tinkled. A little old woman in slippers entered noiselessly by another door and he was astonished at seeing her there in front of him, in the shadows, on the other side of the counter.

She did not ask him anything. Perhaps she was afraid of him?

"May I use the phone?"

He smiled at the thought that she knew him to be a murderer. He went into the booth.

"Hello! Is that Dr. Fisol's house? Dr. Fisol? I should like— Yes. At Madame Couderc's. The widow Couderc, at the Gué de Saulnois. Hello! You know where it is? Yes, I think it's pretty urgent."

He took the occasion to buy some cigarettes, and as he came out again he met the children on their way to school whom he had overtaken on the towpath.

Going back, he counted on seeing Félicie, but there was only old Couderc seated in a chair, on the left side of the door, a cap on his head, heedless of the drizzle. His attitude recalled that of a dog whose owner has chained it up near the door and comes for an occasional glance to make sure it has not got loose.

"He's going to come, Jean? You explained what it was for? You must go down and milk the cows. The poor creatures haven't stopped lowing."

"Of course. Don't be afraid."

"Listen from time to time in case I call. It would mean I was getting worse."

He started by lighting the fire to make himself some coffee and he thought he understood the state of mind of those hundreds of thousands of women who get up early, while the household is still asleep, who move about in their kitchens, rake out the stove, and, to make the coal light quicker, pour some kerosene on it.

He did that too, and a not unpleasant smell pervaded the room while blue flames leaped up. He worked the coffee grinder, and his mind was almost as empty and untroubled as his surroundings.

Upstairs, Tati turned over in bed from time to time. He took her up a glass of sweetened coffee.

"D'you think it's all right for me to drink it? Look at me. Do you think I'm still swelling? Hurry up and milk the cows, Jean."

He sat down on the old man's three-legged stool. The cow's tail made his task more difficult, and he wanted to tie it up; but he could not find a rope. The dung was warm beneath his feet. The animals turned their heads around to gaze at him in surprise.

What was he to do with them now that they were relieved? They must be hungry.

"Jean! Jean! Come up a minute."

He knew she was listening to every sound, following all his movements by ear.

"You'll find some stakes in the shed, near the old gig. There are some chains there, too. I don't know where the mallet is, but it can't be far away. Open the gate for the cows. They'll find their own way to the meadow the other side of the bridge. Tether each of them to a stake, and leave them plenty of chain."

Things were already becoming more difficult and he was worried. Would these big creatures with the staring eyes obey him? He followed them. He had found a stick in the kitchen. He looked in the direction of the pink-tiled house where the old man still sat near the door, and hoped that Couderc would instinctively come to his aid.

He felt clumsy. The grass was wet and he hadn't worn his sabots.

"Come here, cow. Don't be afraid. Why do you look at me the way the shopwoman did this morning?"

He wondered whether Félicie was not behind the curtains, watching him carry on, perhaps making fun of him. When he got back to the house, mallet in hand, the doctor was knocking in vain at the door—a skinny little man in spectacles.

"No one at home?" he shot out irritably.

"There's Tati. I'd gone to take the cows to the meadow."

The doctor did not seem to find the homely smell of the kitchen to his liking and he set down his case on the table.

"Have you any boiled water?"

He soaped his hands slowly, carefully, and, when he wiped them, it took a desperately long time.

Not one superfluous word. Disapproving glances at all that was within reach, at the creaking staircase, at Tati's room, at Tati herself, who watched his approach with terror.

"Can't we have more light?"

"I can light an oil lamp or a candle," said Jean. "There's no electricity."

"Open the window."

Then, as Jean remained standing at the foot of the bed: "What are you waiting for?"

Perhaps this was the doctor with whom Billie's husband had spent the Sunday morning?

Jean took the opportunity to go and look after the chickens and the rabbits. He had to go to the end of the garden to cut grass, and he thought he heard moans.

When he returned, he heard nothing more. Upstairs, the window was still open. Finally, he wondered at the silence, and then he caught the purr of a departing car.

"Are you there, Jean?"

And then, as he entered the room: "My poor Jean. I wonder how you're going to manage. It seems I've got to stay in bed for at least a week."

"What's your illness?"

"He didn't say. He left a prescription on the table. He wanted to know how it happened. I told him I'd fallen going down to the cellar and hit my head on a bottle. Have you given the hens their mash? When you went to the village just now, you didn't see Couderc?"

"He was sitting outside the door."

"They're keeping an eye on him," she said with satisfaction.

"They know that if they let him out of their sight for a moment he'll come back here. He'll come back anyway! I know him! Now, about the prescription. Listen. Go up to the main road. When the bus comes by, give the prescription and some money to the driver. Take a hundred francs out of the soup tureen. If you went to St. Amand yourself, I wouldn't feel right, all alone in the house...."

She was less frightened by her swollen head, now that the doctor had been to see her.

"Look, Jean! They're sure to have seen the doctor leave. They must be wondering what I told him. If I'd wanted, I could have had them put in jail. But I'll get them some other way. Go and see."

"See what?"

"What they're doing. No need to talk to them. On the contrary! They've got to sweat with fear. Pretend to tether the cows farther off."

He waited at the drawbridge for a barge to pass and it slid by very close to him, right at his level, with a young woman at the tiller knitting, a sack over her head because of the rain.

From then on, everything had the same fullness, soft, delectable, and warm. It seemed as though the minutes, like the imperceptible raindrops, were settling cautiously on creatures and things.

Félicie was standing near her grandfather. She saw Jean and he observed that she followed him with her eyes. He had forgotten the mallet. He had to go back to the house for it. He led his cows a little farther away, with the thought that by the end of the day they would be close to the brickyard.

As for Eugène, he had posted himself near the lock, beside the lock-keeper, and they too were looking his way.

Eugène did next to nothing all day long. His job of watchman was a fiction. But he took himself seriously. In the village bar he talked loudly, banging the table with his fist, his bulging

eyes staring everyone down as if to say: "Who dares to argue?...
Who dares contradict me, Eugène Tordeux? Eh?"

From early morning, the white wine lit up his eyes. He
treated his women, as he called them—Françoise and Félicie—
roughly. From his chair, he'd lash out, "I want my pipe."

Like a man who has achieved so much, who bows under
such a burden of responsibilities, that the whole world is duty
bound to help him and spare him any extra effort. He'd spit far
and wide. And utter occasionally, without anyone knowing
what it referred to, "A fine mess!"

And from time to time, when he got out of bed on the right
side, he'd deign to dig a little of the garden. Even so, he would
at once start calling out, "Françoise!...Félicie!...Somebody!...
Bring me the wheelbarrow. Go and get me the rake, you
loafer!..."

Tati was right: they were afraid. Françoise heaved great sighs as
she moved about her kitchen, and the baby had been put in a
corner of the floor, on a blanket.

"What's he doing, Félicie?"

"He's moved the cows. Now he's going back to the house."

"Is he looking this way?"

"I think so."

"What's his manner like?"

"Nothing special."

"Your father should not have done it. He says nothing for
years on end, and then, when he does lift a hand, he—Félicie!
Suppose you went for a little walk that way?"

"D'you want me to speak to him?"

"I don't know. I don't feel right about it. Seeing how she's
called in the doctor."

Jean could guess all that. He did not think much; just bits of
ideas now and then, not necessarily related to one another.

If he wanted to eat potatoes, he had to peel them. Why not? He settled himself near the open door, as Tati would have done, as all women do in the country except in winter, when you sit close to the fire. The brass pendulum swung to and fro with a muted sound. It was already eleven o'clock. He must put more water in the incubator. Then, at midday, he had to watch for the bus to get the medicines.

No one passed by on the path. The soil, normally white in the sunshine, took on the warm hue of overbaked bread and red slugs traced their furrows on it. Now and then a leaf, in the hedge opposite, tilted over and let fall a great drop of water.

He had already peeled three potatoes. He dropped them into a bucket of clean water, as he had seen others do.

Feeling that someone was in front of him, he looked up and saw Félicie, who could barely keep from smiling, despite her worry. Was she going to speak to him? He too wanted to smile. It was just about the first time he saw her without her baby in her arms and she seemed not to know what to do with her hands.

"My aunt's no worse?" she asked at length, putting on a grave air.

"She's not too well."

"The doctor's called, hasn't he? What did he say?"

"He wrote a prescription."

He realized that she was glancing into the kitchen and that she was surprised to see it tidy. She had nothing more to say. She did not know how to leave.

"Jean! Jean!"

A call from upstairs. Tati had heard voices. He got up, and two potatoes rolled onto the floor.

"Who was it, Jean? It was her, I swear."

"Félicie, yes."

"It was her mother sent her. They're scared stiff. You didn't tell her it's not serious, I hope?"

"I told her things were worse."

"Why did you speak to her?"

Poor Tati! She was so ugly in this state! She knew it. She was unhappy. And yet she could not help herself from darting at him a glance charged with jealousy.

"You didn't tell her anything else?"

"No. You called and I came up at once."

"What were you doing?"

"Peeling potatoes."

She was touched. Then suddenly a thought made her sad.

"You'll get fed up, won't you?"

"With what?"

"You know what I mean. You shouldn't be doing this. And to think I'm the one who. . . ."

She wanted to cry. She was sweating in her untidy bed, amid flannels and bandages.

"I've thought of something else. I've been thinking about it ever since this morning. When your father knows you're here. . . . And he will know! Your sister did, and she lives at Orléans. He'll come to get you. He's too proud to accept his son being. . , ."

Suddenly she put a question she had doubtless long had on the tip of her tongue:

"Why did you do it, Jean?"

"Do what?"

"You know what I mean. You got out of the bus and you helped me carry the incubator. Then you stayed. And now . . . And I go on being familiar, I don't know why. . . ."

"You're being silly, Tati!" he shot out, to hide his embarrassment. "You'd better rest a while."

"I'd like to ask you one more thing. Promise you won't refuse."

"Is it so difficult?"

"No! Promise! You can't know how unhappy I am, all alone,

up here in bed. Try as I can to listen, there are times when I don't hear a sound. . . . You promise?"

"I promise!"

"Not to refuse? Well, I want you to promise that, whatever happens, you won't leave without coming to tell me first."

This time, she swallowed a sob and turned away her huge head.

"I won't try to hold you back. What I don't want, you see, is to wait, to feel the door open downstairs, and to say to myself. . . . You promise, Jean?"

"Yes. Anyway, I've no wish to leave."

"You swear by your mother's head?"

"Yes."

He was a little more sad, all of a sudden.

"You're not disgusted at having to do all you're doing?"

"It's fun."

"And when it isn't fun any more? . . . Go, now. You must be hungry. What are you going to eat?"

"An omelet. Then some potatoes with a slice of ham."

"You can bring me up a little bit of omelet. Tomorrow I'll try to get up. The doctor told me not to move if I wanted to get better."

She called him back when he was already on the stairs.

"Jean! . . . There's something else I wanted to say to you. You're getting sick of me, aren't you? If Félicie starts hanging around you. . . ."

"Don't you worry! She doesn't want to hang around me! She loathes me!"

And he went and put his potatoes on to boil.

He did not always wait for her to call. He would climb the stairs, casually, and open the door gently in case she had dozed off, but every time he was met by her wide-awake eyes.

"I've finished. What shall I do now?"

"Is it still raining?"

"It's more of a mist."

"You want to be doing something? The trouble is, I can't even show you where things are. Do you know, Jean, that nobody else would ever have done what you're doing for me? Not even my own mother, whose only thought was of finding me a job and having one mouth less to feed! And she didn't even take the trouble to find out what sort of a house I'd landed in. Have you ever seen a sulfur duster?"

He shook his head.

"There's one in the shed. A pair of bellows with a long nozzle. There must be some sulfur left in it. If not, there's a box on the shelf. A biscuit box. It's a yellow powder. Don't make a mistake. You fill the container that's against the bellows."

"I've got it. What am I to dust?"

"The vines along the hedge."

He spent part of the afternoon at this. Before now, going through the countryside, he had seen men and women working behind a hedge. He remembered their serenity. He had not known what they were doing. He could only see the upper part of a body, a shapeless hat, and sometimes a pipe which had clearly gone out.

Now it was his turn to be the man working behind the hedge and he knew that Félicie was watching him, that now and then Françoise came to have a look.

The old man, innocently, had gone to prowl around his cows. He had even bent down to shift a stake and straighten a tangled chain.

"Papa!" Françoise had cried.

She'd forgotten he could not hear.

"Félicie! Go and fetch your grandfather. He'd have only the bridge to cross and . . ."

When he had dusted all the vine stems, Jean went into the

kitchen to pour himself a glass of wine which he drank standing by the table.

"Is that you?" Tati called.

"*Every person condemned to...*"

It came back to him, for no reason. And all at once, it weighed on him.

"Hasn't the postman come yet? He usually goes by at three o'clock."

"I haven't seen him."

"I thought I heard him. Isn't there a letter on the table? It's more than two weeks now since I had anything from René. He'd just been in trouble again. Give me a glass of water, Jean. You smell of sulfur. I hope you didn't get any in your eyes? It would smart all night and in the morning your eyes would be red."

"Do you remember what I told you the other day?"

"What did you tell me?"

"When you asked for my story. Well, there was one point, anyway, that wasn't true."

She looked at him apprehensively. Why did he blurt this out, just when she least expected it?

"It's about Zézette. I told you it was on account of a woman. There were even moments when I believed so. But it's not true. I never loved Zézette. Without her, it might not have happened in the same way. You understand? But I would have done something else."

No, she did not understand! What she failed above all to understand was his reason for raking over his memories. The weather was mild. He had been working all day, quietly, as people do in the country, pausing every now and then to rest or just to stare in front of him.

"Yes, I think I would have done something else. Anything! I'd felt for a long time that it had to come to an end. I'd reached the stage of wanting it to come as quickly as possible. Have you taken your medicine?"

"Not yet. I didn't have any water."

"Sorry. I'll go and draw some."

Alone at the well, he repeated, "...something else..."

Eugène, Félicie's father, was no doubt down at the village bar, playing cards, or perhaps talking about himself, and when he came home again, heavy-footed and his cheeks on fire, it would be to swallow his soup noisily and fall into a drunken sleep.

Tati had told Jean the story of the lock-keeper. It was not in the war, but in the colonies, that he had lost his leg. He had bouts of malaria. When he did, he would shut himself up in his room. From time to time he would be heard shouting. Sometimes, when his wife opened the door to ask whether he wanted anything, he'd throw a chair, or whatever came handy, at her head.

"Let me alone, for God's sake, or I'll set the place on fire!"

The bargees knew him well. When they did not see him, they guessed that the bout was on him and worked the lock gates themselves.

His wife never complained. She was pregnant. She was always pregnant, even before the youngest baby was weaned, and she had the mask, as they called it—a large blotch of ugly yellow covering half her face.

"Why do you always think about it?"

Jean gave a start. He was not in the least thinking about what she imagined he was. It made him smile.

"I was thinking of the lock-keeper," he said.

"Is he having one of his spells?"

"No. I was just thinking of him, for no particular reason."

"You're bored?"

"No. I think it's about time for me to get the cows. Tomorrow you'll have to explain how to make the butter."

The transition from day to evening was imperceptible because of the veil spread across the sky ever since morning.

The cows, used to him by now, watched his approach and,

as soon as he untethered them, began to move cheerfully toward the shed.

Why, the rain had stopped! The earth was spongy. He bent down to pull out the two iron stakes and to gather up the chains.

He was surprised to hear a voice, quite close to him.

"Usually, they're left."

It was Félicie. She had come up to him, her body askew because she held the baby on her arm. Fine drops powdered her russet hair. She did not smile, but it was pretty clear she would have liked to.

"That's true," he stammered.

What was the use of taking in the stakes and chains? Was anyone likely to come and steal them?

Straightening himself, and turning toward the drawbridge, which the two animals were already crossing, he murmured, "Thank you."

She let him move a few steps away. She was going home too. Each was going his own way. Yet, she added, "Good night."

He turned around abruptly. Too late! She was already off, lifting her feet high because of the grass.

And he walked more heavily. He stroked the ribs of one of the cows with the end of his stick. The lights were on at her mother's. Couderc's silhouette could be vaguely seen behind the curtain.

For his part, Jean got the stable lantern and lit it.

"Be good, you. I'm doing all I can, you know."

The cow wet his legs and feet, knocked over the bucket twice, while the other watched him and lowed. He had not shut up the hens yet. He must not forget to fill the incubator lamp with kerosene.

And Tati, upstairs, lay in the dark. The evening was cool, the window wide open. Frogs were beginning to croak beside the stagnant ponds left by the Cher on the low-lying land.

"All right, Jean?"

The voice came from far away and high up.

"All right!" he called.

In the dairy there were broad dishes in glazed stoneware. As Jean poured in the foaming milk, he remembered how his sister, as a child, used to go and drink milk fresh from the cow at a farm their father had bought.

Would he sleep better tonight? Would it seize him again, like a neuralgia that comes at a fixed time, as soon as he had lain down under the skylight?

"*Every person condemned to death shall be...*"

He finished his work quickly and lit the lamp, an old fashioned one with a bluish glass base. He shut the door and fixed the chain.

"Is that you?" Tati called.

Yes, of course! It was he!

Entering the bedroom, he detected her eyes in spite of the darkness.

"Shut the window first, because of the mosquitoes. Then you can light the lamp. Have you had anything to eat?"

"Not yet."

"Was there much milk spilled?"

So she had heard the bucket upset twice!

"No, not much."

"I'm not finding fault. I know you're doing everything you can. You've not forgotten the incubator? I'm wondering how we'll manage about the market on Saturday."

"I could go."

She touched wood, just as he lit the lamp. It frightened her to talk of a future so distant. Who knows whether by Saturday...

"You didn't see Félicie again?"

"No."

He had not hesitated. The lie had been instinctive, and no one could have been more surprised than he was.

"Her parents ought to put her to work. She doesn't do a

thing all day long. Of course, neither does her father. And Françoise hardly more. They're the sort of people who'd rather crawl with vermin than do anything about it. They think the world owes them a living, and that's a real Couderc way of looking at things. They've just barely enough to eat. And not often meat, at that! Yet they're prouder than if..."

She wondered at the silence enveloping her.

"What are you doing?"

"Nothing. Just listening."

"My chatter bores you, eh? But if you had come into this house at fourteen, like me.... I didn't play with dolls much, I can tell you. It was Tati, here! Tati, there! And carry up some water! And take down the buckets! And go to the shed and see if...! It was always Tati, the softie! And the two girls getting as fat as big slugs and never turning a hand. What are you going to eat, my poor Jean?"

"I don't know. I haven't given it any thought yet."

"Tomorrow the butcher will be going through the village. Just get yourself some meat. For tonight, there must still be a couple of cans of sardines in the cupboard. Take one. Bring me only a bowl of milk with a dash of coffee. I'm afraid of not sleeping."

Going down the stairs, Jean thought: "So am I."

But he took comfort by telling himself that tomorrow would be another day, a soft gray day or a day of sun, both were good, and that he'd light the kitchen fire, then grind the coffee, that he'd go to the shed where the cows would annoy him with their tails, and that finally, when he tethered them in the meadow, Félicie would doubtless be at her door, or on watch behind the curtain.

As she had bidden him good night, she would bid him good morning. She was not altogether tamed yet, but she was beginning to trace ever-narrowing circles around him.

He ate by himself at the foot of the table. He warmed up

some coffee for Tati. Then he lit a last cigarette and climbed up to his loft, which was damper than on other days. The bed-clothes were a little clammy. He curled up in his bed. His eyes were wide open.

He kept wondering whether it would seize him again. He did not want to think about it.

"*Every person condemned...*"

Down below, Tati did not sleep either. There was no one in the old man's room. Who was Couderc sleeping with down at his daughter's place, where there were only two rooms?

The frogs croaked louder than ever. If he thought too much, he would get up and walk in the garden. No—Tati would be scared, she would think he meant to leave.

Would his father come? Tati had thought so. She might perhaps not be wrong. He had always known his father with the gray hair that suited him so well. Now it must be white. But his face must have remained young, with that special expression, that sparkle, that slightly ironic gaiety which are the mark of the man who lives for women.

His sole interest had always been women, all women, and he had spent his life moving from the warmth of one bed to the scented warmth of another, enveloped always by the stale breath of love.

"Are you asleep, Jean?"

She had called softly, but he had heard.

"Almost!" he answered sincerely.

"Good night."

Félicie too had said good night to him. What could a girl like Félicie think of him, knowing that he had killed a man? And how had she come by her baby? Who had fathered it? Where?

He seemed to hear the cheerful voice of his lawyer, fresh from the barber's, with talcum powder behind his ears and his skin smooth and pink, booming at him, "Well, old man?"

"*Article 314 of the Penal Code...*"

"No!" he cried out as in a nightmare.

Realizing it, he wondered whether Tati had heard. No doubt she thought he was dreaming aloud, as children do.

The frogs...Hadn't he forgotten the kerosene for the incubator?...What had she told him?...Oh yes!...The butcher ...in the village...It was his day to call....He had to buy some meat....

They did not eat any meat, at Françoise's, because....

"Good night!"

...But she had already turned away....

...Cock-a-doodle-doo!...

The sun was very pale, almost white, over the skylight, and Tati was stirring in her bed.

8

FIRST the woman in mourning, dignified and disdainful, then the woman from the shop, her neck swathed in medicated wadding. She had lost her voice, that morning.

Then came Félicie's turn. There were others, coming out of nearly all the nearby houses and making for the butcher's truck. They took their time. Many of them, their stomachs swaying in front of them, waddled like geese and ate as they walked.

The rear of the truck, when it was let down, revealed a sort of shop, with quarters of meat hanging from hooks, the scales, the brass weights, and the squares of brown paper hung up on a string.

"Who's next?"

Between two customers, the butcher would blow a little trumpet blast and look toward the upper part of the village to make sure everyone had heard him.

A few drops had fallen again, but it was not raining now. Félicie had come in sabots, a red shawl over her blue smock, and she was carrying an oilcloth bag.

On seeing Jean come up to the van, she had given a little smile. He was the only one not to realize how utterly unexpected he was! As much in himself as in the minor details of his appearance or manners.

He was striding up. He had hurried, because he had seen Félicie at the far end of the towpath. As he was not wearing a hat, his hair was disheveled. He had not shaved. He was on the thin side, and his face was rather reminiscent of an image of Christ.

He did not walk like other people. He seemed to be going nowhere. His arms hung down. In his canvas shoes, he made no noise and his gait seemed all the more lithe. The blue daub of his trousers. The white daub of the shirt he had washed but not ironed.

He found it quite natural to be there, to wait his turn, to glance at Félicie from time to time, then to turn shyly away.

"Eight francs fifty, my pet.... And now, young lady?"

"I want some stewing meat. Not more than a pound. How much is it?"

"Four francs a pound."

In astonishment Jean looked at the scrap of blackish meat, just skin and bone.

"Five francs."

And she, simply and firmly:

"I only want four francs' worth. Cut some off."

She had the two two-franc pieces ready in the hollow of her hand. She paid, swept Jean with a brief look, and went off in the direction of the canal, clacking her sabots as she went.

"And what would you like, young man?"

"A steak."

"How many for?"

"One."

"You like it thick, I bet?"

"Yes, fairly thick."

He was in a hurry. He watched Félicie as she went along, without realizing that the old gossips were watching him, rather as they would have watched a strange animal.

"Eight francs."

It startled him. Eight francs for his steak and only four for the stew that was to be eaten at Félicie's, where there was her father, her mother, and old Couderc.

"You're forgetting your change."

"Oh yes . . . sorry."

"You're welcome."

As he dared not run, he did not overtake Félicie till halfway home. A barge drawn by a donkey was coming from the other direction, and a tiny girl, almost a baby, led the donkey.

The tiller must have been lashed, for no one was to be seen on deck. The canal was quite straight, with, just above, a long stripe of sky between the foliage of the two ranks of trees. And there was not a soul in sight, apart from the little girl and the donkey.

"Why did you run?" asked Félicie, without turning her head, as he fell into step with her, his breath coming noisily.

"I didn't run."

He had nothing to say to her. He craved to be near her, but he had never thought of saying this or that. As he walked, he observed her profile and noted that her lower lip was full, almost swollen, which gave her a reflective, even a pouting, look. She also had a very white, very fine skin, like all red-haired women, and very tiny ears.

It did not embarrass her to be thus inspected in detail. She walked at her own pace and they had covered a good two hundred yards in silence when she asked, as if summing up her thoughts:

"What makes you stay on at my aunt's?"

He did not pause to think even for a second. Indeed he was as much surprised at the promptness of his answer, for he had never asked himself outright.

"I think it's the house."

And she, after another silence: "I wonder what there is so special about that house. Everybody's after it. My mother. My aunt Amélie."

"What about you?"

"Me? It's all one to me."

And, as they approached the lock, she observed, "Why! There's someone at my aunt's."

"How can you tell?"

"You can see the shadow of a car in the path. You'd better hurry."

There was indeed a car. Jean did not recognize it, and was worried. As he entered the kitchen, he bumped into a man who was just finishing drying his hands, and he recognized him. It was the doctor from St. Amand.

"I didn't know you would be coming this morning," Jean said by way of excuse.

"It isn't you I come for."

"How's Tati?"

"Bad."

He must be like this with all his patients. He took real pleasure in saying unpleasant things and, doing so, his eyes gleamed behind his gold-rimmed spectacles.

"Is she really bad?"

"Yes, she's really bad. By the way..."

He was tidying up his bag.

"I must ask you if you intend to stay here."

"But...why?"

Was not the question very like the one Félicie had put to him, only more contemptuous?

"It's none of my business. Though, in a sense, it is my business. Madame Couderc will have to stay in bed for weeks and she will need care. I understand that, apart from yourself, there's no one in the house and that she's not on the best of terms with her family. If you were to leave one fine day, I would have to make arrangements, have her moved to the hospital. You'd better answer me frankly. Are you prepared to look after her as long as may be necessary?"

"Naturally."

"It's not very pleasant."

"I don't mind."

"Very well."

He sat down at a corner of the table to write out a prescription.

"Is she in danger?"

"She might not pull through. I'll call again in two or three days' time."

The doctor got into his car without saying good-bye. Jean, for his part, ran upstairs, halted for an instant on the landing in order to banish any trace of emotion.

"Come in!" called Tati. "What did he tell you?"

"Nothing. He's not a talkative man."

"I'm in for a long spell, eh?"

"Why, no. In a few days' time you'll be up and around."

"Why are you lying? You see, you can tell lies!"

"I swear——"

"Don't swear, Jean, else I won't believe you any more. To begin with, he let me know I would be here for weeks. Then, from up here, I can hear everything that's said in the kitchen. Is it true you will stay?"

"Of course it's true."

"You know that it won't be pleasant to look after me. Since yesterday boils have come out all over my body. I think it's the change of life, do you understand? It's the blood. Look at the thermometer. He looked at it, but he didn't say how much it read."

"A hundred and two degrees."

"Did you buy some meat?"

"Yes, I got a steak."

"You didn't meet anybody?"

"No."

"You didn't see Couderc? . . . Nor Félicie?"

He knew very well that she did not believe him. And then came the same question put in a different form.

"I sometimes wonder what keeps you here."

He did not dare answer, as he had to Félicie: the house. He preferred simply to look at Tati, smiling and shifting his weight from one leg to the other.

"Just now, when the car stopped, I thought it was your father. I was almost pleased you weren't here. Then I heard someone moving around in the kitchen and pouring water into the basin. I couldn't go down. I waited, my mouth dry. What surprises me is that the old man hasn't come to prowl around here yet. I'll bet they watch him every minute of the day. Did you see to the incubator?"

"I've seen to everything. There's another rabbit littered, and another beginning to make its nest."

"Félicie didn't try to talk to you?"

Why did she force him to lie like a child?

"No, I assure you."

"Do you know what you're going to do? Here, I worry myself to death. René's room hasn't been used since he went away. The window looks onto the canal. There's an iron bedstead that will do if it's put up. Do you know how to put up a bed?"

"Yes."

"In the closet under the stairs, you'll find a mattress and a bolster."

"You really want to change rooms?"

He knew that her object was to keep an eye on him and on Félicie. Her present room was the largest and brightest. Moreover, it looked onto the yard and the garden, so that she could see her livestock from her bed.

"Quick, now! Call me when it's ready."

She did not wait for him to tell her. She dragged herself along, barefoot, draped in a blanket. The room, which had been used to store fruit, was fitted with shelves on all four walls.

"Go get a hammer and pliers. You'll take down the shelves. You can get the bedside table from my room. Look."

And through the open window they saw old Couderc hanging timidly around his two cows.

"He'll end up here. Let him come in without saying anything. Try and get him to come upstairs and I'll see to it that he doesn't go back to Françoise's place. Go get the hammer and pliers."

She sweated at the slightest effort, but she would not stay still for a moment.

"Félicie wasn't up buying meat?"

"I think I caught a glimpse of her."

"You told me a few minutes ago you hadn't seen her."

"I wasn't paying any attention."

He tore down the planks. Holes showed in the wallpaper where the nails had been.

"Push my bed nearer the window, so that I can see their house. Anyhow, so long as I'm sick, they won't be able to do anything. Look! Couderc saw me!"

The old man had indeed looked up, and there he stood, motionless, by the two cows.

"You can go down, Jean. It's time you got your dinner ready. I'm only allowed milk and some vegetable soup."

He thought of Félicie all day long and it was partly Tati's fault, for he could feel that she too was thinking of her the whole time. Whenever he went to move the cows, he scarcely dared turn toward the house in the brickyard because Tati, from her window, kept watching him.

At first, Félicie had not noticed. Her baby on her arm, she had come near Jean and watched him drive his stake into the earth. Perhaps she was about to speak to him when she had looked up, followed his eyes, and seen her aunt at the window.

So, with a shrug, she had gone off. Did she imagine he was afraid of Tati?

"What did I tell you? I knew perfectly well she'd start hanging around you. She does the same with all the men."

And he made an effort not to answer, "That's a lie, Tati. You're saying that to make me dislike her. Even if it were true, I wouldn't mind."

Tati had got him to bring her a stick which she kept propped against her bed all day. When she needed anything, she rapped the floor with it. If he was outside, she cried in the high-pitched voice of a mother calling her child, "Jean! . . . Jean! . . ."

And he was embarrassed, because Félicie could hear.

"Do you know who's just bicycled to their place, Jean? Look. The bicycle's leaning against the house. It's Amélie. She's come after the news. She must be wondering what I'm going to do. Look! There she is at the door."

The distance between the two houses—Tati's big house and Françoise's little one—was perhaps two hundred yards as the crow flies. Françoise watched Tati's window. Tati watched Françoise.

"I wonder if she'll dare come."

Amélie did come, balancing uncomfortably on her machine, which she evidently did not often use.

"If only she could fall into the canal. Stay here, Jean. I wouldn't put it past her to take advantage of my being in bed to——"

"Are you there, Tati?" called a voice from the kitchen.

"As if she didn't know I'm here!"

"Can I come up?"

"Come up, you bitch!" growled Tati between her teeth.

"Now, then, what's this I hear from Françoise? That you're ill? That the doctor has called twice already? They say it's the blood?"

Tati did not invite her to sit down and continued to look her sister-in-law in the eyes.

"How will you manage to take care of yourself alone? I hear Father has decided to live at Françoise's. You must allow it's natural he'd sooner live with one of his own daughters."

"Give me a glass of water, Jean."

"We were wondering, Françoise and I, what ought best to be done. Don't you think you'd be better in a nursing home than alone in a big house where anyone can get in while you're lying in bed? I know you won't like it, but, if I were in your place——"

"I'm not alone."

"For the moment! But who's to tell you that you won't be from one minute to the next? One fine morning there you'll be waiting, and the bird will have flown. And you'll be lucky if he hasn't carried off a few little keepsakes."

"Jean!"

"Yes."

"Throw her out, will you?"

"I can leave quite well by myself. . . . Oh well! You've been warned. Now, if anything happens to you, you'll know where the blames lies. As for Father, he asked me to bring back——"

"He didn't ask you a thing. Jean! You're to stop her going into the bedrooms and taking anything whatever."

"But you're surely not going to leave our poor Father without so much as a shirt."

"Show her the door, Jean! She makes me tired. Take my stick. Don't be afraid."

"Good-bye, my girl!"

"Yes, good-bye."

And, once more, they saw Amélie on the towpath, this time returning to Françoise's.

"What did I tell you, Jean? They're trying everything they know to get me out of the house. If I was silly enough to leave for just one hour, I should find them here when I got back and they'd slam the door in my face. What are you looking at?"

"Nothing."

She looked too, and saw Félicie standing at her door. She realized that the instant before the girl and Jean had locked eyes across the space.

"Swear there's nothing between you two."

"I swear."

"Swear you don't love her."

"I don't love her."

Nevertheless, that very evening he was sure of the contrary. He thought of nothing else. At times it was childish. Like a little boy trying to play truant, he elaborated plans to meet her without being seen by Tati.

It was while he was tending the rabbits that he discovered the window in the wall of the shed. Strictly speaking, it was not a window, since it had no panes. It was a hole in the wall, fitted with two bars. To reach it, he had to climb on something, and he set two rabbit hutches one on top of the other, making sure they were stout enough.

In this way, he was below Tati, a little to her left. Watch the canal as she might, she could not see him.

He stayed nearly an hour, at twilight. It was cool and Félicie wore her red shawl again, but in the blue of evening the red became richer than it had been in the morning.

She was taking a stroll, perhaps purposely to meet him. She was not carrying her baby on her arm. She knew that her aunt was at her window, but she did not yet know where Jean was.

So he put a hand between the bars and waved, without imagining for a single moment that it might look ridiculous. She saw the hand. He felt sure she saw it, for she paused. He thought she smiled, a little smile at once amused and content.

Then, almost at once, she turned around and went home, walking slowly, swinging her hips, and not forgetting to stoop and pluck a piece of grass to chew.

"Thank you, Jean! I don't disgust you too much? Not a pretty sight, a woman, eh? Don't you think it odd that your father hasn't come yet?"

"He won't come."

"Well, I think he will."

Poor Tati. The house was becoming her fortress, and her bedroom, with its window ever open on the canal, her watchtower. From morning till night she was on the alert, aware of every sound, starting if she heard a car on the main road, wondering if it would turn into the hazel-lined path; then if she lost track of Jean for an instant, listening to the silence in an anguish of terror that nothing would come to break it.

"Where were you?"

"I was hoeing the potatoes. This morning I saw that the lock-keeper was spreading some stuff on his."

"They ought to be spread with weed killer, too. Do you know how? Somebody came to see Françoise just now. Somebody I don't know. As for Couderc, he very nearly crossed the bridge. It wasn't for lack of wanting to that he didn't. Françoise came and took him back just in time. Have you seen Félicie?"

"No."

"She must have walked this way, because she crossed the lock. The trouble is, I can't lean out of the window. Weren't you speaking to someone, fifteen minutes ago?"

"No."

It was the truth. He had spoken to nobody. But Félicie had walked along the path, no longer on the other side of the water, where Tati's gaze could follow her, but on the track that passed in front of the house. And Jean was behind his bars. He had shown her both his hands less two fingers. Had she understood? He had pointed out to her, insistently, the gate to the left of the house from which he had removed chain and padlock.

Unfortunately, that evening, at eight o'clock, Tati, as though mysteriously forewarned, chose to be attended to. He did not even know whether Félicie had come walking near the gate. If she had, what had she thought?

He lived with her presence from morning till night. He carried the image of her, the thought of her, through the house, across the yards, the garden, into the shed, by the poultry, and by the incubator. Above all, that fullness of her lip haunted him, and her trick of curving her body when she had her baby on her arm.

"What are you doing, Jean?"

"Nothing! I'm tending the rabbits."

He tended the rabbits often, so that he could look through the hole in the wall, and that day again, and the next, he displayed eight fingers with an insistence which must really have been funny.

Had she understood? Was she making a fool of him? When she got home, did she not declare to her mother, "He signaled to me again. I think he's going off his head."

And Tati, every time he went up to her room, searched his eyes as though she hoped to find some clue in them! What clue, of what, could there be in his eyes?

"I was thinking that Saturday you might go to market instead of me, but I'm frightened to stay alone in the house. I'll get Clémence to come up, the one who lives on the right of the path. You know, the little house with the blue gate. If her sister-in-law's better, she can take the eggs and the butter."

She wanted to find out if he would give a start, or show some sign of pique or ill-temper, for then it would mean he had arranged to meet Félicie in town.

However, it came about at a time she had not foreseen, and in circumstances that Jean had not imagined either. When he displayed his eight fingers between the bars, he had no idea what would happen if Félicie did come at eight o'clock. All he knew was that this was the sweetest moment of the whole day, so sweet as to be almost sad, with the canal dropping off to sleep, as things took on their setting of shadow and the red shawl assumed a special quality in the blue and violet of the newborn night.

In the hutches beneath his feet the rabbits were indulging in noisy antics, and now and then a hen shifted on a perch in the henroost.

He did not know what day of the week it was. He had just eaten, alone in the kitchen. From the foot of the stairs, he had called up to Tati, "I'm going to look at the animals."

He had got as far as the garden, among the potatoes, when suddenly he saw Félicie less than a yard away from him.

She was the one who had waited. He could not see her eyes—only her shape. She said nothing. He said nothing either and, quite naturally, as though it had been agreed upon long beforehand, he took her in his arms and kissed her mouth to mouth.

And she had not offered the least resistance. She had not been surprised. As soon as he had clasped her in his arms, she had let herself go limp and, under his kiss, her lips remained submissively parted.

Jean's first thought was that they could not remain there, standing among the potatoes, and he led her gently toward the shed, aimlessly still, and still without speaking. Then he kissed her once more and he saw that her eyes were closed, her neck of an unreal whiteness.

It was, truly, as though it had been foreseen from all eternity that they would meet on that evening, at that spot, and that they need say nothing to each other, that they would recognize each other and have only to fulfill their destiny.

At the moment, Jean did not even know upon what he laid her down: it was hay set ready for the rabbits. And, lying down, she remained inert, while he sought the touch of her flesh. Then, all at once, without thinking, with a dreamlike ease he possessed her.

She clenched her teeth. The rabbits were fidgeting a few inches away from their heads. The incubator lamp, in a corner, gave out a faint yellow gleam, like the vigil light in the vast dimness of a church.

She shook her head to warn him that she could not breathe, so closely were his lips welded to hers, and it was as touching as holding a bird in one's hands, a quivering bird that makes timid efforts to escape.

Then with one shudder she stiffened and, the next instant, her whole body relaxed.

And he stammered, "Félicie!"

He felt that she had opened her eyes, that she was looking at him, with some astonishment perhaps, and that she was trying to get free.

She stood up and shook from her dress the twigs of hay she could not see in the dark.

And, listening intently, as he remained awkward before her, she murmured, "I think you're being called."

Those were the only words she spoke that evening. When she turned to go, he grasped her hand. She abandoned it to him, but she evidently did not feel the need for such a gesture and she wondered still more when he brushed the tips of her fingers with his lips and stammered, "Thank you."

There was a noise from the house. Tati banging on the floor with her stick.

"Are you there, Jean?"

"Here I am!"

He would have liked to look at himself in the scrap of mirror in the kitchen, but the lamp was not yet lit.

"What are you doing?"

"I'm coming."

As he climbed the stairs he ran both hands over his face as if to restore his features to normal.

"What were you doing? Light the lamp."

"I was tending the rabbits."

He took off the chimney of the lamp, turned up the wick, and struck a match. His fingers still shook a little.

"I thought there were footsteps outside. Like someone moving on tiptoe."

He did not answer.

"You haven't seen anybody?"

"No."

"If you could know how afraid I am, Jean! You're getting tired of me, eh? In the end you'll loathe me."

"Of course not!"

"To think that a woman . . . and above all that Félicie."

Why did she mention Félicie just at that moment? She was very red. Toward evening she always ran a temperature and her face appeared more swollen. He looked at her cheek, with the spot that resembled a bit of fur. . . .

"I don't know what I would do, but . . ."

Jean's body threw a large shadow on the wall, a shadow reaching almost to the ceiling, and in the wallpaper the holes showed where he had torn down the fruit shelves.

"You're not bored?"

"No."

"Do you think you can stick it here long?"

"Of course I do!"

"That's what I don't understand. When I saw you come back, along the road, I was almost expecting it, because I took you for a foreigner, a sort of Polack, and those folks, far from their own country, need to find shelter——"

She broke off and he did not notice.

"You're not listening?"

"Yes, I am."

"What was I saying?"

"You were talking about the Polack."

And, smiling dreamily into space, he bade her good night, groped upstairs to his attic, where he threw himself down fully dressed upon his bed.

9

ONE SECOND...two seconds more and he began to suspect that it was a dream.... He tried to carry it through to the end, not to hear the drops of whey falling one by one from the udder-shaped white cheese. In spite of himself, he opened his eyes on the two oblong panes of glass, blue as slate, forming the skylight under which he lay.

He remained a long time as though stupefied, numb, at once ill-tempered and still trembling with ecstasy. The most extraordinary thing was Tati's presence. Looking at their embrace in the way she looked at her chickens or rabbits, with a happy, encouraging smile, and saying, "Love each other well, my pets."

Impossible to say just where all this was happening. It was not in a bedroom. It was not in the shed, either. The light was so bright that it might be the firmament itself, and their pulses throbbed to the rhythm of invisible music, as though a hundred violins sought to exalt the lovers.

He wondered whether, in his dream, Tati had had the bit of fur on her cheek and he could not remember, nor could he remember her clothes, except for the gaudy pink of her slip. As for Félicie, she had pressed against him with such ardor....

His eyelids stung as though a tear were welling up under them. Suddenly, he felt that it was beginning again, that the anguish was stealing over him, would fill his breast anew with a wave of agony.

"Oh, God, grant that . . ."

He sometimes spoke like this, half in earnest, when, in his bed, he felt too much like a little child.

"Grant that I may go back to sleep. Grant that I may have no more nightmares."

It was too late, he knew.

"*Every person condemned to death shall . . .*"

No! That did not frighten him anymore. It was already far away. From moment to moment, his head was clearing more and more, so much so that he could lie down no longer and sat up, wide-eyed, in his bed.

What would have happened if, a short time before, when he was in the shed with Félicie, her father had come in? Or if Tati, despite her illness and her boils, had come downstairs in her felt slippers?

What would he say to Félicie when he saw here again? Who knows? Perhaps she would come back on other evenings? Already he could no longer do without her. So, inevitably, one day or another . . .

He recalled a moment of his life, a moment as airy-light as when he stepped out of prison. It was summer. The examinations were drawing near. The classroom windows were open. The English master looked like a malicious puppet.

Jean had raised his hand, as if asking to be excused. The English master had shrugged. Jean had snapped his fingers.

"Well, what do you want? You need not ask my permission to leave the room, since I regard you as not present."

"I would like to go home. I don't feel well."

He was not yet sure, but he decided to be ill. Alone, he crossed the courtyard and, through dozens of open windows, the voices of teachers and pupils flowed out. In the street, a streetcar shaved past him. Before going home, he went to eat ice cream at Pitigrilli's—three, one after another, despite his temperature.

For less than nothing, he might have dropped his books on

the pavement. It did not matter anymore. He would not be learning any more lessons. He would not be taking his examinations.

When he came out of prison, he had also gone to eat ice cream. They handed him some money, two hundred–odd francs—he did not know exactly why. He had taken a bus. He had slept in one town, then in another, he was committed to nothing, nothing he did possessed either weight or importance.

Tati's house might have come out of a child's building set. He looked at the ancient gilded calendar as one looks at a curious old print. He sniffed the good smells of kitchen and shed. He puttered about, unhurriedly, lighting the fire, grinding coffee, milking the cows, mixing the chickens' mash. . . .

And yet, at eight o'clock, in the darkness of the shed . . .

Alone in his bed, he smiled bitterly. It would start all over again—real life, complications, and, as always, he'd be the one to bear the brunt of fate. He was sure of it.

As sure as when, in Paris, he had met Zézette and entered her apartment for the first time.

He lay down again, did not find sleep, got up, and, barefoot, walked around the loft a dozen times, wondering the while whether, down below, Tati was asleep.

He was dreadfully tired. Not only because of the past, or the present, but because of all the complications he could foresee; he was already growing sentimental over the days he had just lived. He was quite clear about it. Twice, and twice only, in the whole of his life, had he known this innocent peace; once when he'd been ill and ceased to consider school a reality; then again here, this very morning, as he strode toward the village and waited with the gossips behind the butcher's truck. . . .

"Jean! . . . Jean! . . ."

He could tell that he was being called; he did not know

where he was, did not realize that he must get up; on the contrary, he was sinking deeper into an iridescent morning sleep. And suddenly his door opened.

"Monsieur Jean . . ."

A strange voice. A woman he had barely seen, the one who lived in the little house with the blue gate beside the road. She was young, but two of her front teeth were missing, spoiling her looks.

"It's about the butter and eggs you were to give me. . . ."

She watched him jump out of bed in a beam of sunlight. It was late. It was the first time he had awakened so late, having only dropped off to sleep at first light.

He went to Tati's room.

"Didn't you hear me calling?"

"I'm sorry. I slept very heavily."

"Give her the eggs and butter quick. Go with her as far as the bus."

He felt heavy, thick. Always that vague sensation of disquiet, even of anguish. He looked around him as if wondering from which quarter the blow would fall on him.

"Is it bad, Tati's illness?"

"Yes . . . I don't know. . . ."

The hazel-lined path had the smell of damp woods. Now and then, he still tried to recapture remnants of his dream. Félicie must be surprised not to see him yet. He must hurry up and milk the cows, and tether them outside. He had not the heart to make any coffee. He would merely take a glass of white wine to wash out his mouth.

He helped the woman to hoist the baskets into the red bus and watched stupidly as it left.

When he took the cows to the meadow, Félicie was at her door, her baby on her arm, and he thought she made a little sign to him. He turned toward the window. Tati was there, her long and stringy graying hair hanging down over her nightgown.

It would be so easy to live the life of his dream! It would only take....

"Are you coming, Jean?"

He did not know that the postman, who on Saturdays made his round earlier than usual, had already been there. The postman had called out, and started up the stairs.

Now, Tati was holding a letter.

"Come in! I've had news from René. Do you want to read it?"

She too was anxious. He did not want to read it. He took the sheet of paper simply to be polite.

Dear Mom,

That lousy sergeant of mine had managed to put me in the clink again and that's how it will be till it finishes me....

The handwriting of a child, and many mistakes.

The other men have a wife in Paris or the country and get up to a thousand francs every month, so they can wet the N.C.O.s' whistles....

"Money, always money!" sighed Tati. "Every time he writes to me, it's to ask for money and it's no use anyway. Why don't you sit down? You seem so absent. You haven't had a letter, have you?"

She reverted to her first train of thought.

"It's for him I've done everything that I've done, lived worse than a slave, denied myself everything. So that one day he wouldn't be stark naked in the world. And yet there are times when I wonder..."

It was odd: the day when Jean was depressed, she too was sad, and it would not have taken much to make her cry.

"I've got money put by. It's hidden in the house. There's more than you might think. Twenty-two thousand francs."

Her eyes were fastened on him, watching for some reaction, but he was listening to her words without paying attention to them, without taking their meaning.

"Twenty-two thousand francs that I've saved sou by sou, ever since the first day I walked into this house. I robbed them all, the whole lot of them! I cheated, I pinched a franc here and a franc there. Well, not long before what happened to him, René . . . Are you listening, Jean?"

He shook himself, saw old Couderc prowling around the cows.

"I don't know why I'm telling you all this. Perhaps because I've never been able to talk to anybody about it. René was drunk. He came in very late, past midnight. He wanted to go off to South America. His friends must have put that idea in his head.

"'Hand over your money!' he said to me. 'It's no use to you, but I . . .'

"I refused. I tried to calm him down.

"'Drink a cup of coffee, René. You're not yourself.'

"'You think I'm drunk? I'm telling you, I want the money and then I'm off, this very night.'

"He started searching the house. He kept talking to himself. Swearing. I didn't dare leave my bedroom, and he came in again.

"'Now you're going to tell me where you hid the stuff.'

"Believe it or not, Jean, he hit me. That night, I feared the worst. I wondered whether he wasn't capable of murder. . . .

"It was a near thing, but I managed to push him out of my room and lock the door. Going downstairs, he fell, and the next day there was a lump on his forehead."

Jean knew quite well that Tati did not tell him all this without good reason. She was looking at him far too attentively, as she did when she had an idea at the back of her head.

"He's always being punished, and I wonder whether he'll ever come back."

He guessed vaguely. All this meant, confusedly: "...While you, my dear, you're here and you won't go away."

She sighed, asked for a glass of water which he went to get from the well so that it should be cooler.

"Stay with me a little longer. Nothing needs doing in a hurry this morning. Since I've been in bed, I've spent my time thinking. I had to reach forty-five to spend whole days in bed. Before that, sick or not, I kept on going like an animal. What are you thinking about?"

"Nothing."

"No regrets?"

"What?"

"You know what I mean. Now about those twenty-two thousand francs, guess where they are."

He shuddered. He would have liked not to hear the rest. He had the uncomfortable feeling that she was trying to tempt him.

"You go to bed right close to it every night. You've only got to stretch out your hand as you sleep. The dummy. You know? When you unscrew the foot, you find a hollow space inside. That's where it is."

Well, had he been mistaken when he woke up in the night, before the end of such a lovely dream? It was starting! It was starting all over again!

"I'll tell you what I've been thinking. It's about the house. If you don't agree, I won't mind, see?"

A glance toward the brickyard.

"Sit down! When I'm lying in bed, I can't bear to see some-one standing. You seem too tall. Take the armchair. Go on. Come closer. What's the matter with you this morning? You seem upset. Is it because I look horrible? I'll soon be better! Don't you worry. They're not going to get me yet.

"How much do you think a house like this would go for at an auction?"

"I don't know."

"What with the land and the costs, it would bring around a hundred and twenty thousand. You mustn't forget that I come in for a third share, at least I do when Couderc's dead, seeing I'm his daughter-in-law and was married under community-property law. So it's as if I had forty thousand francs of my own. Do you follow me?"

"Yes."

"Forty thousand and twenty-two thousand, that makes sixty-two thousand. More than half the sale price of the house. Now suppose I get a bank loan, or a mortgage for the balance. I know it's difficult...."

Now she was going about it more cautiously, with quick, anxious, piercing glances.

"Suppose someone backed me with a guarantee."

He still did not understand.

"You told me you'd never claimed your mother's legacy. It's none of my business. The law is with you.... If you're angry, say so at once and I won't go on...."

"I'm not angry."

"You'd keep the papers until I'd paid everything back. So you run no risk. Now listen to what comes next. I've given it plenty of thought, you see, and I'm no more of a fool than the next woman. At the market, they all laughed when I bought an incubator. Just let them wait and see. Here, we're short of land...."

"But suppose, while we're buying the house, we bought the brickyard too...."

He quivered and looked automatically at the pink-roofed cottage.

"To begin with, that rids us of Françoise and her brood. They'd be forced to go away because they would never earn their living around here; they're too well known. The brickyard would go for a song. Hand me the magazine lying on the chest of drawers."

It was an agricultural monthly. She showed him whole pages of advertisements about purebred poultry.

"We buy a big incubator that'll take a thousand eggs at a time. Instead of selling the chickens at market we send them all over France, in little cardboard boxes. Look, here are the boxes."

"Yes."

"I'm not asking you to answer at once. You've plenty of time to think it over. You're really not annoyed at me for talking about this? I said to myself that, if your father should come sometime soon. . . . For the time being, *they* won't dare to do anything. As long as I'm in bed and bear marks, they'll be too frightened I might take them to court. Look! There she comes again to snap her fingers at me under my own windows. . . ."

He leaned out and saw Félicie strolling jauntily along the towpath, her baby under her arm. She looked like a little girl playing dolls, an impudent little girl who takes a delight in exasperating the grown-ups.

Her nose in the air, she was looking at her aunt with a smug smile and when Jean appeared she blinked two or three times by way of bidding him good morning.

"Don't look at her," said Tati. "She'll be thinking you're in love with her! She runs to a man like a heifer to the bull and —— What's the matter?"

"Nothing!"

"Is it because of what I said about her?"

"No."

"Because of my plans for the house?"

"No, I'm tired."

Tired, nervous, anxious, sick, as he waited for what could not fail to happen. Tati could never understand. And yet she, too, seemed to have a sixth sense.

"Are you interested in her?"

"Who?"

"Félicie, as you know very well."

"Haven't I already told you, no?"

What possessed her to keep harping about Félicie? Wasn't it she who in the end prevented him from thinking of anything else?

He went downstairs to split wood, angrily. He almost wanted to cut his hand, just to see what would happen. The doctor would have to be called in; perhaps he would have to be taken to the hospital.

Who would answer his call for help, with Tati in bed?

He went to shift the cows. Deliberately, Félicie came wandering near him and he thought she was going to speak to him, even though Tati never lost sight of them.

He almost hoped she would not come that evening. At the same time, he wanted her to be there. He tormented himself, as though wantonly.

"Jean!"

"Yes. Here I am."

"Remember that you're to go down to Clémence's after the baskets and the money."

He went. He did everything that was required. He cut grass for the rabbits, cleaned out the pigeons' cages, and spread manure among the strawberry plants.

Tati was quite capable of calling him precisely at eight o'clock. Would he go up? She didn't call and he was half disappointed.

It was already five minutes past eight when he made his way toward the garden, and he found Félicie sitting calmly on a shaft of the cart.

"She runs to a man like. . . ." Tati had said.

He wanted to talk to her, to sit down beside her, to put his arm around her waist. Best of all would have been for the two of them to stroll along the canal, arm in arm, listening to the frogs and breathing in the peace of evening. He said, without thinking, "You came."

And he had scarcely brushed against her when she let herself go in his arms, her warm mouth glued to his mouth.

He was embarrassed. She was limp, as though unconscious. Waiting. They were at the very same spot as the evening before. He thought that her father might have followed her, that Tati was capable of coming downstairs. . . .

She had shut her eyes. On his lips was the taste of her mouth and in his nostrils the smell that went with her red hair.

She gave a little sigh, like the sigh of a child. She stiffened in anticipation. She clenched her fingers around his wrist, trying to dig her nails into his skin.

"You're hurting me!" she said softly. . . .

The evening before, it had all gone with such marvelous ease! Now he was clumsy, without desire. He was annoyed with the rabbits for stirring close to their heads. He was annoyed with the straw for rustling, with the voices that came from a barge moored at the lock where the bargee's family were taking the air.

Afterwards, there was a silence, and then Félicie asked, "My aunt hasn't said anything?"

"No."

"She must suspect something. The way her eyes followed me all day long. . . ."

She got up, satisfied, though perhaps not fully.

"Do you mean to stay with her?"

"I don't know."

"I must go home. My father might . . ."

She turned back to give him a little kiss at random on his face. Then he heard the squeaking of the gate hinges. He looked up and was surprised to see that the sky was all stars.

He was so weary that he sat down on the shaft of the cart

while Tati, worried, got out of bed and dragged herself along on her huge legs, calling continually, "Jean!...Where are you?"

A candlestick in her hand, she started downstairs. He was surprised to see a strip of light under the kitchen door, but did not wonder why. He was away, far away, in an almost astral world....Invisible currents bore him along, tossing him about....He'd go forward....Slip back....And the waves reunited him with Félicie for an instant....He clutched at her....He clung....

Already he seemed to feel contrary currents.

"What are you doing, Jean?"

Tati sighed with relief at finding him alone.

"I was wondering whether you'd gone. Why, the very thought of it...I think it would be even more dreadful than if René..."

She left unfinished what seemed to her like a blasphemy.

"Aren't you coming in?"

"Yes."

"Help me. I thought myself stronger than I am."

In the darkness, she gave off a smell of bed, of ailing flesh, of medicine.

It had been so wonderful when he got out of the bus, there in the sunshine! And when he had discovered the house, with all the little cares that it demanded and that took up the whole day!

"It's silly of me. I thought you weren't alone. I don't know what I should have done. I..."

The wave, now, carried him back to the kitchen, then to the narrow staircase up which he had to push Tati, and into her bedroom, where he closed the shutters.

And then, there was nothing but to go back to his loft, though he knew that he would not sleep, that he would be assailed by his terrors while Félicie, quiet and sated...

She probably let an arm hang down as she slept, with her

bosom clear of the bedclothes, and he was sure that a smile sometimes crossed her face like a breath of wind over water, that her lips moved without uttering a sound.

10

TATI SWORE that the summer was spoiled. Every two days, every three days at most, a storm rumbled in the distance, without even bringing a cooling shower. It could be felt far off in the air, somewhere in the direction of Morvan. The atmosphere was heavy. The rays of the sun, suddenly, seemed painted in oils. The thunder would crash at the four points of the horizon, wrinkling the water of the canal, and the chestnut leaves trembled, the skirts of cycling girls billowed, a few drops fell, almost reluctantly, and then came hours of gray gloom, of gusty wind, of mist.

It had happened for the first time on a Sunday, and that time Jean had laughed, almost wholeheartedly.

The morning had still been sunny, though a trifle hot, and except for the time he'd spent tending the animals, he had spent it in Tati's bedroom. Quite recent events already wore the charm of memory as though he knew that they would never come again. For instance, that first Sunday when, after the midday meal, they had sat outside the door, by the road. Tati in a wicker armchair, knitting, himself astride a straw-bottomed chair. He'd been smoking that pipe of old Couderc's, which he had cleaned out with brandy.

"That makes a week today I've been in bed!" she observed, looking at the dark hole formed by the doorway in Françoise's white house.

He looked too. He noted that houses, in the country, always have their doors open.

"Otherwise," he thought, "there wouldn't be enough light.... The windows are too small."

At that hour, Félicie would be dressing for church. Jean was sure she washed in the kitchen, where she would set the bowl of soapy water on the floor to soak her feet. The baby too would be on the floor, dirty as always. Eugène, on Sunday and on Sundays only, as though too hard-worked during the week, was in his bit of garden. As for the grandfather, he was waiting his turn to be washed and to be dressed in black, with his white tie and his elastic-sided shoes.

Was it for Jean that Félicie had brought, or made a new dress? An apple-green dress. As soon as she left the house, she looked toward the open window. Doubtless she saw Tati's head in the foreground. Did she make out Jean in the half darkness behind?

She went off along the towpath. Tati observed Jean, who pretended to think of something else, and she sighed.

The people outside, not knowing there was going to be a storm, prepared to spend a Sunday like any other. Some settled themselves along the canal; others, with packs on their backs, rode far afield on their bicycles.

"You could have killed a chicken," said Tati suddenly. "Life hasn't been much fun for you this week."

They never ate chicken in this house devoted to poultry rearing, because they preferred to sell them. Tati thought of that.

"If you talk to people about me, they'll tell you I'm stingy. That's because they don't know what it's like to spend your life as other people's servant. If I'd treated myself to dresses like that female, I wouldn't have saved a sou and I would be risking...."

Yet, Félicie had disappeared; her green dress had long since been swallowed up in the two rows of greenery which met at the horizon. But Tati followed her in thought. Perhaps in Jean's thoughts?

And now voices were heard on the path.

"Why! The bus has gone by," she observed.

Then she cocked an ear.

"I think. . . . Yes . . . that's Amélie's voice."

Soon they saw the family on the bridge, the father with straw hat and pince-nez, the little boy in a sailor suit, and Amélie, who carried with great care a box of pastry. The little boy turned around. Still looking straight ahead, his mother gave him a good shove, forbidding him no doubt to look at that house.

They were going to Françoise's house. The old man was ready, washed, spruced up, and a pipe was put in his mouth; he was being settled outside—as if nailing him there—in a ray of sunshine. Françoise alone still had to wash. She put up her hand to shade her eyes, saw the family coming, and no doubt exclaimed, "Eleven o'clock already!"

Whereupon she hurried indoors and tidied up the front room.

"Before, they never used to see each other," Tati observed. "Désiré thinks he's brainy. He looks with contempt on Eugène and his wife. But, when it's a question of hatching a plot against me. . . ."

They brought the table outside. Désiré, who had taken off his jacket and whose shirt sleeves gleamed like snow, helped Françoise, but the table was wide and could barely get through the door.

Félicie came back from church and glanced up at the window. She had a red flower on her new dress.

They spread a cloth on the table, brought some chairs.

"She's killed a rabbit," Tati went on, never letting them out of her sight.

And they, eating the rabbit, pretended to be mighty busy, but couldn't help stealing glances at the window. Only Eugène used his pocket knife to eat with. Amélie had brought an enormous creamcake.

It was exactly when she started cutting it, not without pride, that the first flurry ruffled the water, and all at once the foliage began to quiver so hard that leaves were snapped off. The tablecloth lifted. Drops of rain fell.

Jean laughed heartily. It was fun to see them scramble up, to see Amélie rescuing her cake. Désiré, who didn't know what to do and was hunting for his jacket, which he had left indoors.

A fine rain fell all afternoon and they had to remain in the kitchen, sitting in a semicircle around the door. At five o'clock Amélie, her husband, and the little boy left. They had borrowed an old umbrella under which they huddled together, heads bowed, in the wind.

Would Félicie come all the same?

Firecrackers sounded far off, followed by detonations, and now and then the breeze brought gusts of music from the hurdy-gurdy.

"I'd forgotten it was the fair today," Tati murmured, glancing quickly at Jean. There must be a shooting gallery, a merry-go-round, a floor and a band for dancing. . . .

Was that why Félicie stayed so long on the doorstep looking toward the house? She finally donned an old raincoat, with a hood, and went off toward the village. She was going dancing. Perhaps she hoped Jean would follow her?

Instead, he floundered in the slimy mud of the yard where everything was soaked, and he had scarcely done tending the animals, was still looking bitterly at the spot where Félicie ought to have come to meet him, when Tati called, true to the craze, the obsession it had become, "Jean! . . . Jean! . . . What are you doing?"

More firecrackers went off in the wet night. He heard them

from his bed. He even saw gleams that doubtless came from a wretched fireworks display, and he thought he heard the outlandish strains of a trombone, a fiddle, and a piano.

From then on, no two days passed without a storm. For one thing, the weather took a long time to improve. The sky remained a greenish gray and the waters of the canal were restless. The leaves dried gradually. In the mornings, the atmosphere was rather clearer. There seemed to be some hope that summer would begin again, but all at once, between noon and three o'clock, the rumblings would sound in the distance.

Félicie came on the Monday. The rain had stopped, but it had fallen all day. The hay gave out a strong smell. Jean was cross.

"You went dancing?" he asked, groping for her in the dark. "What time did you get home?"

"I don't know. Past midnight."

"Who did you dance with?"

"All the boys."

"And you didn't do anything else?"

She laughed, but did not answer. He was unhappy. She did not realize what a price he was paying for her.

"Jealous? You mustn't . . ."

She offered her moist lips.

Ever since he had possessed her in his dream, he failed to find the simple pleasure of their first embrace. It had gone so naturally! Now, they looked for a place. Félicie settled herself.

"Wait a minute. . . . There . . . Come on now. . . . Don't squeeze me so tight."

One day, Zézette had said to him with a sigh, "It's just my luck! I wanted to stand myself a gigolo, and I'm landed with you—a fake sugar sou."

Because he was jealous! Because he would not let her pay when they went out together! Because he insisted on keeping her although he could not afford it!

"You didn't do anything, last night, with anybody?" he asked Félicie in a murmur.

"Of course not! Why?"

Was she already tired of coming to him at eight o'clock every evening? The next evening she asked him, "Are you really going to stay here long?"

"Why?" he replied.

They exchanged so few words, yet even those were too many since, when they did speak, the words did not fit.

"I don't know. For my part, I'd sooner live in a town, or somewhere just outside Paris...a little three-room apartment with peace and quiet. A job where you draw your money every Saturday...."

Was it an invitation? He made no answer. Everything irritated him, everything distressed him, even unexpected details: "No. Don't...We can't today."

Well, wasn't that precisely the occasion for her to nestle in his arms, her cheek against his, whispering away in the dark?

"It's time I went home. If you don't see me tomorrow, it'll be because my father..."

The doctor came to see Tati and looked at Jean as though he found it astonishing that he was still there.

"Is she any better?"

The doctor shrugged.

And, all day long, Jean trailed around in the mud in Couderc's overlarge sabots. Everything was soaked, slimy. He got dirty doing nothing at all. To go and shift the cows, he put a sack over his head and shoulders. And only rarely did he see Félicie framed in her doorway, where Françoise, on the other hand, planted herself constantly.

Tati, upstairs in bed, was fretting. She could not let an hour go by without seeing him and, as soon as he came in, she would look at him intently as if to read on his face the news of disaster.

"Getting bored? You weren't made for the countryside, eh?"

"On the contrary. I've never been so happy in my life."

He said it in a mournful voice, for by now it was no longer true.

"Do you know what I sometimes think? Now don't get angry.... It would be better for us both if you were really a Polack. Do you remember? I asked you if you were French. I took you for some foreigner or other.... When you told me who you were, I didn't believe you."

She reverted to her ruling idea. "It's odd that your father hasn't come."

And then, distrustfully: "You're sure he hasn't? I've written to a lawyer at Vierzon, whose address I found in the paper. To ask him how to go about getting the house."

Exactly like Zézette, who, one fine evening, had announced, "I've found an apartment."

And he had to rent it! And that flat had been like the starting point of what had happened, because he had needed to borrow money that very day!

"We'll be in our own place—what you want so badly."

"Yes. In our own place..."

Félicie dreamed of a three-room apartment in town!

From morning till night, Tati devised plans to get Françoise and Félicie out of the way for good!

As for Jean, he moved about in the midst of things that already had no more than the value of memory—the calendar, the stove he lit each morning, the table in the light of the paned window, the portraits of Couderc and his dead wife, and...

It would have been so simple! They would have lived here, all three of them, or rather all four, since there was the baby. He didn't mind the baby. He did not wonder whose it was. It fitted into the scene as he imagined it. Old Couderc too, if need be! Why not?

They would live, like that, all together, tending the poultry and the rabbits, hatching eggs, cutting grass, sowing vegetables.

Tati would shout, as she was wont, "Jean! Bring in some coal."

And he would get coal from the shed.

"Jean! We're out of wood."

And he would chop wood, with the ax which, in the early days, he had hardly dared handle.

He would see Félicie playing with the baby in the grass, going down on all fours and crying, "Look out! The big wolf... the big wolf... the big wolf!"

The baby's laughter. His mother's laughter as she stood up in the grass, with her blue smock and her tousled red hair, and freckles all around her eyes.

"Love each other well, my pets!"

Now and then, at the muggy hour of the siesta, Tati would go up to her room followed by old Couderc and dole out pleasure to him as one gives a lump of sugar to a dog.

On Thursday, Félicie did not come and he remained alone in the shed for a good fifteen minutes. When he went up, Tati guessed right away that he didn't look like himself.

"Where have you been, Jean?"

"In the garden."

"What were you doing?"

"I don't know."

He wore a guilty look, when on that particular day, in fact, he was not guilty! Yet this was the day she chose to be suspicious. The window was open.

The storm still rumbling along had not cleared the air, but an occasional gust of wind made the curtain swell and set the lamp smoking.

"You're sure you were alone?"

"Yes."

"Why don't you sit down? You've got something on your mind, haven't you? Is it because your father doesn't come to see you?"

"No."

"Is it because you're tired of looking after me?"

"I——"

"Are you bored?"

"No."

"Is it on account of Félicie?"

Her gaze grew sharper and Jean tried in vain to appear natural.

"Come on, admit that you think of nothing but Félicie. You do! I've seen it all right. And she—well, she hangs around you. She's smart! Instead of crossing the bridge, knowing I'd see her, she comes over by the lock gate so I can't tell where she's going. Félicie was in the garden with you?"

"No. I swear——"

"Because I'm going to tell you something. Listen...I shouldn't talk this way. The other day, I let you know I had some savings and I purposely told you where they're hidden. That's something I wouldn't have told even René...."

Of course! Of course! He knew he meant almost more to her than René did. He had somehow taken René's place, with a few things added.

"Well, if you had left, and taken the money with you.... Don't get angry. You didn't so much as think of doing it, I know that. But if you had, I wonder whether I'd have been angry with you. Even now, you could say, 'Tati, I'm sick of it all. I must go away.'"

It happened quickly. He saw her throat rise. Her illness made her ugly. But she became uglier still when, her features melting into one another, she began to weep, her face screwed up like a child's.

"Don't...don't pay attention....There! Give me a handkerchief....You...you'd want to leave that...."

But beneath the tears her face already resumed a harshness and she was sitting up in bed.

"Only, there's one thing I'll never forgive, never allow, which is that you and that girl I loathe. . . . You see, Jean, if you did that. . . . When I think how all my life those people have. . . . "

She could not find words strong enough.

"I don't know what I'd do. But, stuck here in bed or no, I think I'd have the strength to get up and. . . . "

She tore her hair in rage and impotence.

"If you went after another girl in town, for your fun. . . . But Félicie! . . . You don't answer?"

"No."

"You love her?"

"No."

There were only the two of them in the house, in the drafty bedroom. They could be seen from the other side of the water. Probably no one was there to watch them? Félicie had not come!

In the house in the brickyard they were in bed. It must be warm there. There were four of them breathing away in two tiny rooms and Eugène's breath was strong, reeking of liquor.

"Yes . . ."

It was Jean who had just said yes after having said no. He was conscious of having registered a deed of utmost importance. He had said yes because he no longer had the courage to deny, to keep up the farce, to go up to the loft, and there, alone in his bed, to be siezed as on other nights by cold sweats, waiting for what could not fail to come to pass.

"Jean! What did you say?"

She could see he was not himself. He was too calm, his look withdrawn.

"Jean! You love her?"

"Yes."

"And you've slept with her?"

"Yes."

He smiled timidly, as if to apologize.

"Jean! It can't be. Tell me it's not true....Jean!"

She had thrown back the bedclothes. Her bandages were bared. Never had he noticed so clearly the bit of fur on her cheek.

"Don't leave, Jean! Listen!...I must explain....You must tell me....How could it have happened?"

Why upset herself like this? Was he getting worked up? His head was clear, perfectly clear! He could see every detail of the room, including the curtain billowing as if there were someone behind it; he got up to turn down the wick because the lamp smoked.

"It happened in the shed, near the rabbits."

"Listen, Jean. I'll go down on my knees. Do you hear? I'll grovel at your feet. I know I'm an old woman, a pitiful old woman with no right to hope....But if only you knew....All my life..."

She was on her knees, on the floor.

"Don't look at me like that....Listen...."

How was he looking at her? Calmly. Never had he looked at her so calmly.

"Just promise me not to see her again. I'll make them leave. I'll find a way to make them leave..."

"*Every person condemned to death shall be...*"

He smiled a pallid smile.

"Why are you smiling? Am I so silly? I'll do anything you want. I'll give you....Listen! The money I told you about...Take it! It's yours! What am I saying? Don't smile...."

He was not smiling. It was a twist his lip took of itself. He was sad, really. Or rather morose.

Since it had to be, he accepted the inevitable. She had ended up by clutching his leg and she still groveled on the floor, while he thought he could hear a voice reciting:

"*Men condemned to forced labor shall be set to the hardest possible work; they shall wear an iron ball at their ankles...*"

Of course! Of course! It was the only thing to do! He had

known it for a long time! It had been foreordained! And was it not the simplest way?

"*Any murder committed with premeditation or preceded by ambush is defined as assassination...*"

He had not premeditated it. It was not his fault! And there was no ambush....

"I'm not feeling well, Jean. Help me to get up, to get back into bed.... You absolutely must understand. Ever since I was fourteen..."

What about him?

"What are you looking for?... Jean! You frighten me.... Jean! Look at me. Say something to me...."

"What?"

"I don't know.... I...Jean!"

He had found the hammer, the hammer he had brought up when Tati moved into the room and he'd pulled down the fruit shelves.

"Jean! I beg you...."

What good would it be? It would only start all over again! And then again, and again! He had had enough.

"I've had enough! Enough! Enough!" he shouted suddenly. "Do you hear me? Do you hear me, everybody? I've had enough!..."

He had struck perhaps three or four blows on the skull bruised as it already was, when he began to wonder, with Tati lying inert before him, whether Françoise's people had not heard him shout. He went to the window, his hammer in his hand. He saw that no light showed in the house in the brick-yard. It was raining.

Tati was still moving slightly. She had kept her eyes open.

Wearily, he struck two or three more blows, then, grabbing the pillow off the bed, put it over her face.

His knees trembled. His mouth was dry, and there was an emptiness in his chest.

This time, he was familiar with the Code. It made him almost smile and it was half aloud that he recited Article 314, the famous article that had given Maître Fagonet such a deal of trouble.

"Murder shall entail the death penalty when it precedes, accompanies or follows another crime."

This time, he would not need to lie. Unless he took the money hidden in the torso of the dressmaker's dummy....

Who knows? Perhaps they'd put him in the same cell?

Zézette had come to see him once, in the visiting room. Would Félicie come too?

He left the lamp alight, went downstairs in the dark, and felt on the mantelpiece for matches. His hand encountered Couderc's pipe. He wanted to smoke a pipe. But first he must have a drink. He was thirsty. He was hungry.

He lit the lamp. He noticed that the pendulum of the clock was about to stop and he carefully wound up the brass weight.

There, that would do for another eight days!

He cut himself a slice of ham, opened the cupboard to get out some bread, and frowned as he thought he heard a noise up above.

No! She was well and truly dead!

It was all over!

All he had to do now was to eat, to drink his bottle of white wine, smoke the old man's pipe, and wait....

The rain was falling outside, pattering on the leaves, making rings on the surface of the canal. Astride his straw-bottomed chair, he looked in front of him and once in a while uttered words under his breath.

"I'll tell them she did it deliberately ... because she did do it deliberately! ... From the very first day ..."

He was walking along the main road, in the sun, a tiny shadow at his feet, and he moved with easy strides from the shadow of one tree to the shadow of the next, through diamond-shaped patches of sunshine....

He had signaled a car that had not stopped....

Oh well!

Then the big red bus had come panting up the slope...and Tati had looked at him with screwed-up eyes.

Suddenly he got up. He had just thought of something. He opened the door into the yard. A leaden day was breaking. And now he went to the incubator from which came a cheeping sound. Some chicks had hatched. Others were struggling out of their broken shells and yet others were just beginning to peck at their prison walls.

"Tati would have been pleased...."

Was it white wine he had drunk? Two bottles stood on the table, both empty. The second was the bottle of brandy.

"I must go and tell Félicie. It's Félicie who will..."

He fell down, sank into the depths, slept.

And, toward ten o'clock, when the gendarmes arrived on their bicycles, summoned by Françoise, who was worried by the silence of the house, a silence broken only by the lowing and kicking of the cows in the shed, it took them some time to find him, stretched out near the pan he used each morning to mix the mash for the poultry.

He was sleeping, a fly on his cheek, his lips parted, puffed out like a child's, like Félicie's, and from them escaped a breath reeking of drink.

They woke him by kicking him in the face and legs. He grimaced, opened his eyes, recognized the gendarmes.

"Oh yes..." he said, making an effort to get up.

Then he begged them: "Don't hit me...."

And finally, standing, swaying on his feet: "I'm tired.... I'm so tired!..."

Nieul-sur-Mer,
May 1, 1940

OTHER NEW YORK REVIEW BOOKS CLASSICS*

For a complete list of titles, visit www.nyrb.com or write to:
Catalog Requests, NYRB, 435 Hudson Street, New York, NY 10014-3994